A Touch of Truth

A Shade of Vampire, Book 28

Bella Forrest

ALSO BY BELLA FORREST:

A SHADE OF VAMPIRE SERIES:

Series 1: Derek & Sofia's story:

A Shade of Vampire (Book 1)
A Shade of Blood (Book 2)
A Castle of Sand (Book 3)
A Shadow of Light (Book 4)
A Blaze of Sun (Book 5)
A Gate of Night (Book 6)
A Break of Day (Book 7)

Series 2: Rose & Caleb's story:

A Shade of Novak (Book 8)
A Bond of Blood (Book 9)
A Spell of Time (Book 10)
A Chase of Prey (Book 11)
A Shade of Doubt (Book 12)
A Turn of Tides (Book 13)
A Dawn of Strength (Book 14)
A Fall of Secrets (Book 15)
An End of Night (Book 16)

Series 3: Ben & River's story:

A Wind of Change (Book 17)
A Trail of Echoes (Book 18)
A Soldier of Shadows (Book 19)
A Hero of Realms (Book 20)
A Vial of Life (Book 21)

A Fork Of Paths (Book 22)
A Flight of Souls (Book 23)
A Bridge of Stars (Book 24)

Series 4: A Clan of Novaks

A Clan of Novaks (Book 25)
A World of New (Book 26)
A Web of Lies (Book 27)
A Touch of Truth (Book 28)

A SHADE OF DRAGON:

A Shade of Dragon 1
A Shade of Dragon 2
A Shade of Dragon 3

A SHADE OF KIEV TRILOGY:

A Shade of Kiev 1
A Shade of Kiev 2
A Shade of Kiev 3

BEAUTIFUL MONSTER DUOLOGY:

Beautiful Monster 1
Beautiful Monster 2

For an updated list of Bella's books,
please visit www.bellaforrest.net

Join my VIP email list and I'll personally send you an email reminder
as soon as my next book is out!
Click here to sign up: www.forrestbooks.com

Contents

Prologue: Brucella

On arriving at Murther Island, it took a while to figure out exactly how I should approach the Mortclaws, and how I would get them to do my bidding in a way that would leave me alive to tell the tale.

After a long spell of contemplation, inspiration struck me. The perfect idea formed in my head. Clutching the heavy key in my hands, I headed cautiously to the Mortclaws' cave, whose fiery gated entrance was situated among clusters of giant boulders. The depths of the prison were dark which made the Mortclaws hard to spot, given that their coats were also pitch black.

Then I caught sight of gleaming eyes through the bars of the gate. None of them glowed red. . . yet.

I still had no idea how much power they retained after the demise of the black witches. But since it was daytime, and they were all in their wolf forms, they obviously still possessed some extraordinary abilities.

As soon as I had captured their attention, they lunged forward. I immediately averted my vision to the ground for fear that their eyes would turn red and bore holes into mine.

The giant black wolves growled and spat at me, remembering, of course, exactly who I was. They demanded to know why I had come, but most of all they—Sendira, Bastien's mother, especially— were anxious to know what had happened to Bastien. Where he was now, how he was doing, what powers he possessed, and if he was even still alive. They hadn't seen him since he was a cub, after all.

I assured them that Bastien was alive and well. I explained that he displayed symptoms that indicated the black witches had messed with him somewhat as a cub— such as his ability to shift at will— but not nearly as many as the Mortclaw adults. I proceeded to reveal what had happened to his adoptive parents; how they had recently been killed in an unfortunate incident.

Then I told them the reason for my visit. I informed them that I had come to strike a deal — a deal that they would be utterly foolish to refuse. I held up the key to their cave, dangling it painfully close to them, and told them that I would free them, and they could see their long lost cub again... *if* they would first do me two small favors:

First, they would hunt down the human girl who was the main obstacle between my daughter and Bastien's marriage. This condition they were quick to agree on, as none of them liked the idea of their fine boy ending up with such a frail, mortal creature.

Second, they must agree with Bastien marrying my daughter, and Sendira and Vertus would demand he marry her if there was still any reluctance on his part, even after the human girl's death.

My second condition was vital in more ways than one. It would serve not only to secure Rona's marriage to Bastien, but also my tribe's safety after the fact. Once my daughter was married to their son, the Mortclaws and the Northstones would be family. As low as the Mortclaws had stooped in the past, family was one thing I knew for certain that they still considered highly valuable. They would never sink so low as to murder one of their own. Other, non-related wolves? Perhaps. They might embark on a killing spree again if they returned to The Woodlands. I might be responsible for numerous deaths in the near future. The Mortclaws' cannibalistic appetite would be a problem I'd have to solve when the time came. In the meantime, I had to focus on making sure that my conditions were accomplished and the knot between Bastien and my daughter was tied as soon as possible.

Sendira and Vertus growled at my second condition. They made it amply clear that the last thing they wanted was for their son to end up with the daughter of the woman who had been responsible for their imprisonment on Murther Island. I couldn't blame them for their reluctance, but I knew they couldn't refuse. And they didn't. They were far too desperate. If they did not agree to both of my terms, then I would simply leave, and they would be trapped here for the rest of their miserable lives.

Of course... I was not stupid. I was well aware that the Mortclaws' agreement to carry out my requests was a whole different matter than actually executing them. Once I had opened up the charmed gate, and they all rushed out, there would be nothing to stop them from simply attacking me. Eating me alive.

The only way I could think to counteract this problem was to bluff. Bluff with confidence I did not possess. I told them sternly that I was in allegiance with a powerful circle of white witches. The same witches who were responsible for locking them up in the first place. I informed the Mortclaws that the white witches were aware of my coming to see them, and would assume the wolves had harmed me if I did not report back to The Sanctuary in two days' time confirming that I was still alive and safe. If this happened, they would once again hunt down the Mortclaws and imprison them for an eternity.

This was a stretch of the imagination, certainly, but would these wolves really run the risk of getting holed up again in this cave? After all the decades of misery they had spent in this darkness? I didn't think so. I didn't think that anyone, no matter how much they doubted the veracity of my statements, would risk that.

Whatever the case, I was definitely not keen on the idea of letting them all out at once. I proposed to the Mortclaws that I would first let out only one of them—they could decide amongst themselves whom that would be. That lone wolf must fulfill my conditions before I freed the rest of the pack.

The Mortclaws discussed my proposal amongst themselves for a while. Eventually, it was decided that Sendira would be the wolf to complete the necessary tasks.

I was trembling like an animal as the moment arrived for me to finally push the key into the lock and turn it. Before doing so, I instructed all of them to line up at the back of the cave, except Sendira, in case they got any scheming ideas about forcing their way out all at once. I also instructed Sendira to transform into her humanoid form. She acquiesced.

Gulping, I turned the key. I drew open the gate only

wide enough for her to slip out, before slamming it shut again, locking it, and stowing the key firmly within my bosom.

I was hardly breathing as I stared at Sendira standing opposite me. Even though, as a humanoid, she was not oversized like she was while in her wolf form, she was still a much taller woman than me. I dared raise my eyes to meet hers directly. She held a definite look of disdain, but also, undeniable resolution. From her expression alone, I sensed that she was not about to take any risks that I could be lying about my "circle" of witch guardians. As fierce as she had looked in her anger when I'd first arrived outside the cave, there was also a weariness to her countenance.

Understandably, she wanted to begin the tasks immediately. I informed her of my suspicion that Bastien was staying with Victoria in the human realm — specifically, in The Shade. She was already aware of the island's existence, but she did not know its precise location.

I knew that the Mortclaws' sense of smell was unparalleled, stronger than a dozen normal wolves' combined, especially after the black witches' spells. So I told her about the portal on one of the ogres' beaches, through which I was sure Bastien had traveled. Even though days had passed since he must have left the supernatural dimension, I held strong hope that Sendira would still be able to track him down. He was her son, after all. A wolf mother had a way of finding her child against all odds; it was almost mystical. We possessed a bond with our cubs that could never be severed…

Not by a thousand miles.

Chapter 1: Grace

I gazed around the old loft I had woken up in at the top of a dilapidated skyscraper. I was in the middle of a ravaged Chicago, in the epicenter of Bloodless territory.

I didn't know who had brought me here, and I sure as heck didn't know what I was supposed to do now. I had hoped that whoever my savior had been would have shown up already. I had been cooped up here for several hours, and I wasn't sure how much longer my nerves could take waiting.

It was the not knowing that was the worst. Not knowing whom I owed my life to, why they had bothered to save me from that river, and what, if anything, they planned to do with me next.

I had spent as much time as I dared gazing out of the ceiling window, taking in the grim view of the city. But I was afraid to watch for too long in case one of the Bloodless either scented or spotted me. Unlike other inhabitants of The Shade, I had virtually no experience with these creatures. I didn't know exactly how strong their sense of smell was, and even though my blood was half fae, it was half human too. Which meant I was at risk. So I thought it wise to spend most of my time sitting close to the burning, bitter-scented coil.

I couldn't keep track of the time, because, although there was a clock on the wall, its hands had not budged from four o'clock since I'd woken up.

But after what felt like many hours, I couldn't stand waiting any longer. Drawing my knees up against my chest, I rubbed my temples. *Think, Grace. Think.*

I needed to contact The Shade and tell them where I was. There were several phones on the island that allowed incoming calls from the outside—phones that Fowler used to have access to, so that he could contact us to call the League out on missions... in the days when we were still an authorized, official agency. Before joining the League, it was mandatory for all aspiring members to memorize those numbers, so I knew each of them by heart.

Will any phone in this building work? I wasn't even sure if there was still electricity running through this part of the city. I glanced around the loft for a light switch, hoping to test my speculation, but spotted none.

I waited for what felt like another hour and still nobody showed up. I decided it was time to risk stepping outside. The coil was starting to look dangerously close to burning out. I didn't want to imagine what might happen after that. I was running out of time.

Moving over to the coil, I carefully scooped it up into my hands and then picked up a box of matches I'd spied earlier, nestled beneath the gas lantern. I gazed around the rest of the odd assortment of items stashed in the loft, but figured that the coil and the matches were the only two things that would be of real use to me while venturing downstairs.

So, moving to a trapdoor in the far corner of the loft— the exit that I had spent some time hovering around earlier as I pondered whether I ought to leave—I gripped the cool, metal handle and heaved it open. Thankfully, it wasn't too noisy.

I gazed down to see a corridor beneath me. Its floor was covered in a grimy dusty blue carpet, and its walls were grayish—though I imagined they had once been white. There was no ladder or other means of climbing down in sight, which meant I would have to jump. I estimated the leap was over twelve feet, but I had been forced to jump from higher distances before.

It was hard to leap from this kind of height without any noise. I was just lucky that there was carpet beneath me. I landed with a dull thud, and was mindful not to damage the coil. Rising slowly to my feet, I held the burning object in front of me. My breathing came hard and fast as I gazed up and down the corridor, half expecting a Bloodless to come charging toward me. But it was empty.

My first instinct now was to look around for a light switch, to test if there really was any electricity in this building. I found one further down the hallway and pushed it. Nothing happened. *Perhaps this isn't actually a light switch and it's for... something else*, I thought hopefully, even as I doubted this was the case.

I turned my thoughts back to my main problem.

I needed to find a working phone. Unsure of which way

to turn next, I took a right and began to make my way slowly down the corridor. I stopped at the first door on my left, which was ajar. I peeked through the crack first. The room was some kind of spacious office, lined with dozens of damaged tables, chairs and smashed-up computers.

On spotting no signs of life, I mustered the confidence to push the door open enough to slip inside. The cracked windows let in a chilly breeze. I shivered.

There were phones on each desk. Some of their wires had been snapped, but others appeared to be intact. I moved to the nearest undamaged handset and picked up the receiver. The line was dead. I moved to a second phone and picked it up. Also dead. I wished that I could say I was surprised.

I moved to a lamp perched on one of the desks and tried to turn it on. Nothing happened. I checked that it was plugged into the socket—and indeed it was. I could hardly argue that I hadn't turned on the right switch this time. I supposed that the fact that I had spotted a kettle in the loft hideout had given me hope that there was some source of electricity in this building, but perhaps he or she—or they—had just used it as a container.

Electricity was out. Phone lines were dead. I had no way

of communicating with the outside world. At least, not in this building.

I glanced down at the coil in my hands. Still smoking, but for how much longer?

Think!

I moved toward the exit of the office, since this breeze was doing nothing for the longevity of the coil. As I approached the door, I caught sight of my reflection in a cracked ornamental mirror hanging on the wall near the doorway. I hardly recognized myself.

My eyes were bloodshot, and my face, neck and chest were covered in a bright red rash. I examined myself beneath my clothes to see the rash had also spread down to my stomach, thighs, and the upper half of my arms.

It must've been the toxic river water's effect on my body. I prayed that I wouldn't come down with some kind of horrible illness. I hated to think how much of that water I had swallowed when I had been in the grips of its current.

Tearing my eyes away from the mirror, I moved back out into the corridor, looking left and right. Still empty.

What now?

Perhaps going back up to the loft would've been the safest option, but I couldn't bring myself to wait any longer. The silence and solitude had been driving me insane.

Perhaps there would be a working phone in a different building. *Is that really so impossible?* But searching for another phone would mean braving the streets, which I had already witnessed were stalked by gangs of Bloodless.

I knew for sure where working phones did exist, of course. Back in the IBSI's headquarters, on the other side of the river. And behind their HQ, I was sure that there were also regular human residences. But I would be an absolute fool to head back that way. The hunters might be on the lookout for me even now—I had no idea where they were, or what they thought had happened to me.

Hopefully they thought I had drowned. That would certainly be the logical conclusion, after falling into rapids that strong with handcuffs restraining me.

So if I don't head back toward the other side of the river, toward human civilization, where else?

As I stood in the dim, dank corridor, I drew in a deep breath, trying to calm my nerves and think straight. I could not give in to despair and hopelessness.

A moment of clarity came upon me.

I have to find whoever saved me. That's what I've got to

do.

Whoever it was, I supposed they did not wish me harm if they had gone to the trouble of fishing me out of the river and bringing me all this way to shelter—how they'd done that amidst the Bloodless roaming the roads, I didn't know. I shuddered just at the thought.

Would my savior, or saviors, have gone far? What if they were even hanging around in this building somewhere? I needed to explore these floors. Perhaps they had deliberately left me alone so that I could sleep, recover from my ordeal. I comforted myself with these hopeful thoughts as I began moving slowly and cautiously down the corridor.

I wished that I could call out to see if anyone was nearby. But of course, I couldn't. I might as well be calling for my death.

I reached the end of the corridor and arrived at a set of elevators—broken, defunct elevators. Next to them was a staircase, however. I didn't want to think about how many steps I would have to climb down to get to the bottom. This building was so high—I guessed over twenty floors, though my estimation could have been wildly off.

I set the coil down and opened the box of matches,

which thankfully were not damp. Sparking a flame and brewing it in my right hand, I replaced the matches in my pocket, picked up the coil in my left hand and started down the staircase. It was frighteningly dark. I was already imagining myself halfway down the first flight of stairs and coming face to face with one of those pale, nightmarish creatures. I'd never been more grateful for my ability to wield fire than I was then. The flames were comforting, though the shadows they sent dancing on the walls on either side of me gave me shivers. I tried to keep my eyes firmly on the stairs in front of me and quell my overstimulated imagination.

I realized how much I was sweating as I arrived on the next floor down. I exited the staircase and stepped out into another corridor. As I scanned left and right, something caught my eye by one of the doorways. I could've sworn that I spotted a moving shadow. My throat grew tight and I froze, staring at where I thought I'd seen it.

I moved toward the door slower than ever, and peered through the doorway. Another office room. An apparently empty office room.

I'm just getting spooked.

I explored this floor a bit more before returning to the

staircase and making my way down to the next floor—moving noticeably faster this time. I stopped on each floor and explored as much as I dared, but each time found nothing of importance. No signs of whoever it was that had saved me. By the time I reached the ground floor, even my half-supernatural muscles were beginning to feel the workout.

I gazed at a metal plaque fixed to the wall outside the staircase. It had an arrow pointing right. "Reception," it read. And then beneath that was another word with another arrow, pointing down the corridor in the opposite direction. "Parking," it said.

A reception area didn't sound like somewhere I wanted to go—it made me think of some grand lobby with lots of glass windows—probably all smashed, and leading directly into the dangerous road outside. But a parking garage didn't sound much better. Though if it was in the basement, underground, as parking usually was in buildings such as these, maybe…

Given that I wasn't exactly overwhelmed with options right now, I headed in the direction of the parking garage. Indeed, the arrow led me toward a pair of elevators and another stairwell. I reached the bottom of the stairs and arrived outside a thick metal door with a round handle. Gripping it with one hand, I pushed it open to create the smallest crack. I peered through into a pitch-black basement, filled with vehicles. I couldn't see enough through this small gap, however, so I was forced to push it open wider. I stepped inside, holding out my fire and making it flare higher to cast its halo further around me.

Surprisingly, the vehicles were intact. At least, none of them appeared to have any visible damage to them. And indeed this room in general seemed to be quite untouched—which was odd, considering that the door had been unlocked.

I weaved in and out of the vehicles and moved down the center of the parking lot. Reaching the other end, I stopped and pressed my back against the wall to scan the room from this angle. To my right was a slope leading to what appeared to be the basement's exit—a wide, corrugated iron gate. Likely electronic, and I guessed now defunct.

Disappointment swelled within me. I had traveled down the entire building and still not found anyone. Granted, I hadn't felt safe enough to spend much time in each room in order to do a completely thorough search, but if someone was here they should have heard me. *Dammit.* They could have left a note or something for me, even the slightest explanation would have helped—the vaguest indication of when they might return, or even *if* they would return.

My frustrated thoughts evaporated as a scatter of debris fell from the ceiling.

When I glanced up, my heart stopped.

The ceiling.

I hadn't yet checked the ceiling.

CHAPTER 2: GRACE

The ceiling was lined with naked, pale backs. Bloodless.

I'd just walked right into a nap room.

I didn't have time to chastise myself for not having the presence of mind to look up the moment I entered the basement. Heck, I barely even had time to think as the Bloodless that had caused the falling debris—the first Bloodless to have awoken—dropped to the floor ten feet in front of me.

The others—there were maybe twenty in total—were quickly aroused by its motion and the next thing I knew all of them were stirring, their legs lowering and long, lanky bodies dropping down all around me like stick insects.

I was practically choking from fright as I made my fire blaze and spark out toward them. The Bloodless nearest to me let out ear-splitting screeches. At least the flames caused them to step back.

The coil being of no use to me anymore, I hurled it toward the crowd before moving forward, forcing those around me backward. I spun around fast and continued rotating my fire to ensure that none of them caught me from behind.

I had to get out of this basement. I had to get to the exit!

I managed to cause enough heat to pave a path to the door. As my left hand closed around the metal handle, I cast a backward glance. The Bloodless were following me—encroaching as close to me as they dared. I pulled open the door, darted up the stairs and raced down the corridor even as my fire singed the walls and carpet. In my panic, I wasn't even sure where I was heading. Just anywhere away from the loping crowd behind me.

I found myself heading toward the reception area. Reaching a set of double doors whose glass was smashed, I barged into a spacious lobby which was just as dilapidated as the rest of the building. I lunged across the room to the broken revolving doors at the other end and burst out into the frigid street.

I barely had time to think which direction to head in. This street was clear of other Bloodless for now—at least, from what I could see.

Somehow, I just had to get these monsters off my trail… even though they had already scented my blood.

I darted to my right. The sky above was overcast with heavy, black-gray clouds.

If it started to rain, this situation would escalate to a whole new level of desperation.

I raced down the street, my blood pounding in my ears. I reached the end of the sidewalk and took a sharp right turn again, around the corner of the building. When I glanced around me, it was to see that several Bloodless had caught up with me by now, running parallel with me and several feet apart to avoid my heat.

And then one leapt right in front of my path.

Shocked, I stalled before coming to my senses and continuing to surge forward. Would this creature stand getting burned to have me?

Could a half fae turn into a Bloodless? What would I

be, half fae, half Bloodless? I shook the thought aside. I couldn't start entertaining thoughts like these. *I'm going to escape this. I'm going to escape.*

As the Bloodless leapt aside just as we were a few feet from colliding, it appeared that they really were afraid of my fire. They did not want to feel pain.

Thunder rumbled overhead. And then I felt it: the first drop of rain on my face.

Crap.

I could still manipulate fire in rain, but it was twice the effort, and I wasn't sure how long I could keep it up. I wasn't practiced at wielding fire in such conditions. Skirting around the building, I looked wildly around for somewhere, anywhere, I could possibly hide.

I caught sight of an open drain on the other side of the road. Or rather, I smelt it before I spotted it. Its stench was so vile, it stunk up the entire road. As the rain started falling more heavily, I couldn't pause to think. I darted in and out of the broken-down vehicles—many of them strewn right in the middle of the road—to reach the other side. Arriving at the edge of the drain, I leapt into it.

Thick, dark sludge swallowed up my feet, legs, and torso. But my only concern right now was keeping my hands above the liquid. I'd realized too late that dropping down in here would ruin the matches—which were still in my pocket. Now covered in this slime, they were useless. At all costs, now more than ever, I had to keep my fire blazing because if it went out, I would be completely and utterly defenseless.

Left and right of me was a long tunnel—with several more openings at intervals. The tunnel was not tall enough for me to stand to my full height. Bending over, I began hurriedly wading forward.

I'd heard that Bloodless were deterred by very strong, disgusting odors—like the smell of a decaying corpse, for example. The rotten substance surrounding me was definitely a rival to that. It was all I could do to stop myself from vomiting as I forced myself to continue wading forward.

I looked back over my shoulder, praying that I was alone down here... but I wasn't. The stench hadn't worked. Jumping down here and ruining my matches had all been in vain. Maybe they were just that starved for blood that they tolerated the stench.

With heavy splashes, Bloodless had begun piling down into the drain after me.

Now I was in a worse position than when I had still been above ground. Half of me was submerged in this liquid. Half of me, completely unprotected by my fire.

As they moved toward me, I surged the fire in their direction, hoping to scorch at least the first few that led the group, before continuing to hurry onward.

Now, I had to find a way back up. Even if it was raining. Even if it killed me.

Down here was certain doom.

A pale beam of light shone up ahead, trickling down from the road and into the depths of the gutter. I could just make out a ladder leading up to it, attached to the side of the wall. Another entrance to the sewage system. It didn't seem like it was that far, either, but wading through this thick grime slowed me down considerably.

I managed to reach within a few feet of the ladder when an ice-cold, hard, bony hand clamped around my ankle. I screamed, kicking with my shoe as hard as I could. It felt like the ridge of my sole made contact with the attacking Bloodless' face beneath the sludge. Whatever it made contact with, the hand loosened, allowing me to pull away.

I hurried forward with desperation I'd never experienced in my life, but made it only another couple of feet before another hand grabbed me—my left knee this time.

And then, without warning, a sharp pain shot up my left leg. I felt … fangs. Sinking into my flesh. Closing around me. Razor-sharp teeth that felt like sharks' jaws.

One's got me.

One's biting me!

I let out a bloodcurdling shriek as I struggled to free myself, but as I did, the fangs only sank deeper.

"No!" I screamed, as if my volume would save me. "No!"

I kept fighting to pull away while maintaining the fire protecting the upper half of me. But fighting only increased the pain. My flesh tore beneath the monster's teeth, and soon began to sting unbearably from the toxic substance I was covered in.

I was in a state of shock that this was actually happening. A Bloodless had gotten me. Was biting me. *This can't be happening.*

Although any reasonable person should have expected to get caught, I couldn't believe it. I refused to believe that one had managed to latch onto me. Escape was my only option. I would survive.

As another hand gripped my right leg, however, there was no more denying it. And I had no weapon with which to reach them or fight them off. I attempted to manipulate the liquid I was immersed in, make it rise up, reveal the Bloodless beneath it, but it was so thickly polluted with other substances, it was hardly responsive to my powers. I managed to surge up a wave, but the liquid I'd displaced was immediately replaced with more slime, and I failed to scoop deep enough to reach my attackers.

I struggled to keep my head above the surface as a second pair of fangs dug into me.

Feeling myself being pulled under, I gazed hopelessly toward the exit. The ladder—it was so agonizingly close. I made one last attempt to reach it, even abandoning the fire in my left hand in order to get a hold of it. I lunged, my fingers clasping around the cold rusted metal. But I was still stuck, and now that my fire had diminished, more Bloodless lurched for me.

As much as I had learned from my father about tenacity and the will to survive, I couldn't help but think that maybe there came a time when you just had nothing left. When you had to give in. When fighting only prolonged the pain…

A sudden chorus of screeching erupted from behind me and pierced through my desperate thoughts. Then I heard an odd sound… it sounded like the whirring of rotor blades, slicing air and liquid.

Indeed, as I gazed into the darkness, I caught sight of a spinning wheel of blades levitating in the air. Rotor blades. They looked sharp as knives. I stared, stunned, as I realized that they were slashing through the crowd of Bloodless, severing their heads, limbs… rendering the sewer into Bloodless soup.

The blades spun so fast, they spliced the entire crowd of Bloodless in under a minute, until it arrived within two feet of me—me and the Bloodless who were still beneath the slime and feasting on me.

Dizziness was beginning to overtake me, but I just managed to keep my vision focused enough to witness the blades dip beneath the surface. I heard the sound of muffled screaming underwater. The gunk surrounding me churned wildly, and then the fangs withdrew from my flesh in quick succession. The blades started churning up pieces of pale limbs—bits of hands, arms, legs… heads.

Then the deadly wheel lifted out of the slime, only a foot in front of me.

Although my body was begging to just collapse, I finally launched onto the ladder and pulled myself above the liquid. I couldn't yet bring myself to glance down at my legs to see what kind of a state they were in, much less consider what was about to happen to me next. My wounds were stinging so badly, I couldn't help but feel that blood poisoning would end up killing me before turning ever did.

"Hey!" A deep, female voice echoed abruptly down the tunnel.

Then I caught sight of two figures—one short, one tall—wearing dark clothes, gloves, and gas masks covering their faces. Two people whom I could only assume in my dazed state had been my original saviors.

They started wading through the sewage toward the ladder and as they arrived beneath me, I realized that one of them was a man. From what I could see of their faces through their masks—which wasn't much, mainly their dark black-brown eyes—they were young, perhaps in their early twenties. From the similarity of their eye colors, maybe they were siblings.

The girl swore as she looked at my leg.

"Oh, great. They bit her!" she hissed to the man. She

had a New York twang to her accent.

Alarm flashed in their eyes and they began to retreat.

"Wait!" I cried. "Please! Don't leave me!"

I realized that I still had a small spark of fire left in my right palm and I used all the energy left in my worn body to coax the spark into a blazing fire.

"I'm not a human!" I exclaimed. "I am half fae. I may not be affected by Bloodless like normal people!" I struggled to believe my own words even as I spoke them. But they had to believe me. They had to, or they would just leave me here to rot.

They stopped in their tracks and stared at me. Then they exchanged glances.

"Please, help me!" I urged. "I'll do you any favor in return!"

"It's too risky," the girl muttered to the boy after a pause.

The boy's eyes raked me. "But she's not a human," he replied in a low voice. His accent was the same as hers. I also realized in that moment that he was holding something in his right hand—it looked like some kind of remote control… for the spinning wheel? It had to be.

"Half fae," the girl addressed me, narrowing her eyes.

"That means you are also half human, right?"

"Yes," I wheezed, unsure of how much longer I could stay conscious in this agony. "But please, help me."

"She's not showing signs of turning yet," the boy said, doubtfully.

"It could just be slower," the girl shot back. She shifted on her feet impatiently, and then to my horror, stepped back. "Orlando, let's just go."

But the boy—*Orlando*—stayed where he was.

"If she has powers, she could be useful," he replied.

"Useful for what?" the girl responded. "We don't need anyone."

Still, the boy stayed where he was. "Fire is always useful," he replied, even as his eyes settled on me again.

The girl breathed out in frustration. "I don't like this. I really don't like this."

"If she starts turning, we can always leave her behind," he replied. "What's the harm?"

The girl continued to glare at him.

But the boy already seemed to have made up his mind. "Come on, Maura," he pressed. "I said we can dump her if we have to."

Dump me. Like a pile of trash. Not that I could blame

them.

My heart soared with relief as Orlando moved toward me. He wrinkled his nose as he eyed my wounds. Then he said, "Keep your head down."

I wasn't sure why he would ask me to do this, but I wasn't about to argue. I leaned my head closer to the metal ruts of the ladder.

He shifted a dial on his remote and the rotor blades sped up, sending the substance spraying in all directions— including all three of our faces. Only mine wasn't covered by a mask.

The wheel moved past me and tilted sideways before heading up the tunnel above me, through the round sewer hole, and up into the street where it continued to hum.

"All right, it's safe to climb out now," he said.

He gripped the first rung and nudged me in the back to start moving up. Something I didn't exactly appreciate considering how much pain I was in.

Gritting my teeth, I forced myself to climb. As I moved higher, rain began to splatter heavily on my head—rain that was previously a nightmare was now a relief. It helped to wash off the grime I was coated with.

The rotor blades whirred above my head as I pulled

myself out of the drain and rolled out onto the street. I glanced around fearfully for more Bloodless. But this drain was situated in between a large vehicle and a wall, so I could not see if any were approaching yet.

The girl and the boy climbed up next to me. I struggled to rip my bloody lower pants to free the skin on my leg. Orlando assisted me, withdrawing a Swiss Army knife from his pocket. He cut through the fabric, and I had full view of the damage inflicted by the Bloodless. I felt queasy as I stared down at four deep puncture marks that had ripped wider left and right in my flesh—due to my attempts to pull away from the monsters while still in their grasp.

At least I could be grateful for one thing. It seemed that Orlando was correct—I wasn't showing signs of turning… yet. I felt dizzy and nauseous from the pain, and it felt like all I wanted to do was throw up. But I hadn't started shaking yet, and there was no burning sensation running across my skin…

"Well, what now, Captain Genius?" the girl murmured sourly.

"Shut up, Maura," Orlando snapped. "You know what we have to do next." He moved over to me and placed an arm around my waist before pulling me upright.

"It's a serious question," Maura responded, sounding equally annoyed. "How are we ever going to get back with her like this?"

"You can still walk, right?" Orlando addressed me, his dark eyes digging into mine.

I nodded. I could, though it was painful—my legs were not paralyzed.

Orlando turned to Maura. "Then if she can walk, she can glide."

Chapter 3: Grace

"If she can walk, she can glide."

I hadn't the slightest clue what Orlando had meant by that, but I didn't have to wonder long. He kept one arm around me in support while he worked the remote with the other hand. The three of us moved around the vehicle blocking our view and looked up and down the street for Bloodless. There were none that we could spot, but he kept the blade-wheel circling protectively around us all the same. I could only wonder how these people had gotten hold of such a device... and who the heck these people were, for that matter.

They led me to the other side of the road, and we moved down an alleyway. At the end we reached a narrow external staircase that climbed up a gray-walled skyscraper. I stared upward at the building's dizzying height. I was nervous as Orlando and Maura moved me to the first step, and we began to climb.

"Uh, how far up do we go exactly?" I rasped.

"To the top," Orlando grunted.

As we began to climb, from the speed at which they both were climbing, I could tell that they were human. Though my speed wasn't even a match for theirs. Orlando soon realized that he had underestimated my strength as I lagged after the second flight.

"Get on my back," he ordered, turning to me.

"You'd better not slip in this rain," Maura mumbled.

Orlando ignored her comment and helped me climb onto him. He was taller than me, but he hardly felt stronger as I wrapped my arms around his shoulders. His build felt slim and narrow beneath me. As we wound higher and higher, he had to stop more than a dozen times to catch his breath, even setting me down on the steps for a minute or so while he regained his stamina. All the while, the rotor blades followed us.

Finally, we reached the top of the stairs. The rain continued to hammer against us, and a strong wind blew fiercely. I was truly impressed at the craftsmanship of the wheel—how it managed to stay where Orlando guided it, even against this resistance.

When we arrived on a sprawling roof, we were all thoroughly drenched. This meant that at least my wounds had been cleaned, even though I felt frozen to the bone. Worryingly, however, the bite marks were still stinging.

Were the Bloodless only sucking blood from me? Or did they try to turn me?

I didn't know if their biology worked the same way as regular vampires'.

I was distracted from my worries as I gazed around the open rooftop. This was the best view of this wrecked Chicago I'd had so far.

Why had this duo brought me up here?

Had they really been the ones to save me from the river in the first place?

Who were they?

I had so many questions, but now was not the time to ask them.

Orlando lowered me to my feet. They led me toward

the edge of the roof, where a thick metal cable was attached. The cable was strung from this skyscraper to the neighboring one, a street away.

Maura reached for the thick belt wrapped around her waist and unclasped a small compartment at its front, which I had previously assumed to just be a metal buckle. A hook was situated beneath it, and as she tugged on it, I realized that the hook was attached to a wire, about four feet long.

My jaw dropped as she leapt onto the ledge. Crouching over, she fastened her hook to the cable. Then she leapt off, launching into a terrifying glide over God knew how many feet, until her feet collided with the building opposite us. She clambered up over its ledge and rolled over, disappearing from view.

My heart was thumping as Orlando approached the wire. He released the hook from his own belt and proceeded to do exactly the same as Maura. But before he swung off, he cast a glance down at me.

"I can't risk traveling with you like this," he said sternly. "If you want to come with us, you're going to have to do this yourself."

I stopped breathing for a few seconds.

"I'll throw back my belt and hook to you once I'm on the other side," he went on. "Make sure you catch it."

My heart was in my throat as he leapt off and glided the distance to the other building.

I might be half supernatural, but I still had fears. This was… insane.

Now that I eyed the buildings surrounding us, I realized that many of them had cables attached, interconnecting them just like this one. Maybe this was how Maura and Orlando—and whatever other non-Bloodless lived out here—got around. I guessed it was safer than traveling by foot on the ground… at least safer from Bloodless.

As I neared the ledge, it sure didn't feel like there was anything *safe* about what I was about to attempt.

Once Orlando had lowered himself onto the opposite roof, he did as he said he would—removed his belt and hurled it into the air toward me. His aim was shockingly good. It came shooting toward me and I caught it with relative ease.

My hands were trembling as I stood next to the cable. I dared not peer over the edge. I felt vertigo just *imagining* the height without gaining an actual glimpse of the distant ground.

God. Am I really going to do this?

How *am I going to do this?*

But I had no choice. I couldn't stay alone up here on this roof.

I wrapped the belt around my waist and adjusted it to my size. The buckle was already opened, the hook ready to use. One less thing for me to do. *One less excuse to procrastinate.*

I winced and raised myself to the slippery ledge. I pulled out the hook and fastened it to the cable. My palms were sweating as I trained my eyes on the opposite building.

Well. Here goes nothing...

Chapter 4: Grace

I could have sworn that my life flashed before me as I went flying off the roof of the building. For several harrowing seconds, as I rocked violently from side to side from the force of my launch, I feared that I had not attached the hook properly and I was about to hurtle down to the ground in a gut-mangling freefall.

What happened was only slightly less terrifying.

Now that I was out in the open, exposed to the horrifying drop, my eyes could not help but shoot down to gauge the distance. It felt like my heart might stop.

But then my feet hit against the other building,

shooting agonizing pains up my already injured legs. Orlando reached down to me and gripped my forearms. He hauled me upward, over the edge, and rolled me down onto the roof. Onto a beautiful, hard, flat surface. And it was all over.

As he dipped down to detach his belt from my waist, I realized that I was shaking all over—not because I was turning (at least, I hoped not)—but because of the shock. Even the leap I'd made over the IBSI's fence had not felt as scary as that. For one thing, there had been water on the other side.

It took me several moments to regain composure. Breathing heavily, I sat up straight and slopped back my wet hair away from my face. I gazed up at my two companions.

Orlando was in the process of navigating the blade-wheel over to us from the roof we'd just left. And they had both removed their masks. For the first time, I had a full view of their faces. Faces that took me aback. It was clearer than ever that they were siblings—other than their eye color, they shared similar facial features: the same sharp, slightly hooked nose, thin, small lips, and longish faces. But that wasn't why I was gaping.

They were pale. Too pale to be humans. And their skin appeared thin. I could practically make out the veins beneath it, even through the gloom. Their dark hair, which almost matched their eye color, was cropped short. But it looked thin—for both of them. I could almost see their scalps beneath it. And their lips were an odd color—almost the color of someone who'd gotten frostbite. Slightly blue and purple. It struck me all of a sudden just how much their sickly appearance reminded me of Lawrence.

Orlando's brows were heavy and severe, forming almost a unibrow when he frowned, as he was doing now.

"Wh-Who are you?" I stammered.

"There may be time for that later," Orlando replied.

May be time… I found his phrasing discomforting.

"We need to keep moving," Maura pressed.

They both put on their masks after breathing in deep, concealing their faces once again.

Before I could utter another word, Orlando grabbed my right arm and pulled me none too gently to my feet.

Then, to my deep despair, they led me to the other side of the roof, attached to which was another dreaded cable leading to the next roof. Maura mounted it, attaching the hook before launching off and ziplining to the building opposite.

Oh, no.

Orlando seemed to catch the crestfallen expression on my face.

"Yes," he said, pointedly. "We have some way to go yet."

"*Where* are we going?" I asked.

"Back to base," he replied even as he attached his own hook to the cable and launched off.

Where is "base"?

I was leery of anyone using the word "base" by now. It made me think instantly of the hunters' headquarters.

Once Orlando reached the other side, he threw me back his belt. And once again, I was forced to undergo the traumatic process of ziplining from one building to the other. As I hit the other side and Orlando helped me climb onto it, I couldn't help but ask, "Why not just travel on the ground? You have a powerful weapon." I eyed the rotor that Orlando was coaxing along with us.

"It's for use in emergencies," he replied, before the three of us walked to the other side of this third building. "Besides, although it can be effective on small crowds, it's way too risky to rely on for large ones. Sometimes the rotor breaks down."

Large crowds. The crowd that had been chasing me had appeared to be large in my eyes. I dreaded to think what Orlando's definition of "large" was.

No more words were spoken as we continued traveling from building to building. After the fifth stretch, I hoped that I would've gotten a bit more used to it, but each one was as hair-raising as the last. I found myself constantly expecting something to go wrong: for the safety belt to give way, for the cable to snap… Finally, after what felt like over twenty rooftops, we stopped in the center of a roof.

I was still alive. Shivering from cold and still in gut-wrenching pain from the stinging in my legs, but alive.

Relief washed over me as Orlando and Maura did not move to the ledge of this building, as I'd been expecting them to. Instead, they headed to a door, which I guessed led down into the building. It was secured with a heavy-duty lock. Maura withdrew a key from one of the many small compartments in her wide belt and unlocked the door. Orlando lowered the blade-wheel to the floor and stalled it before picking it up. We stepped inside, out of the pounding rain, and emerged at the top of a rundown stairwell whose olive-green walls were peeling. Maura quickly slammed the door shut behind us and locked it again. She began hurrying down the stairs with Orlando following after her. I, however, could not move so quickly. The gliding certainly had not done any favors for my injuries, and I was only able to move at half of their pace. Orlando, appearing quite exhausted himself, did not offer to carry me again. Instead the pair slowed down a little, so that I would not get so far behind.

Thankfully, they stopped after two flights of stairs. We parted from the staircase through a brown doorway and emerged in a narrow hallway, so narrow that it would be a stretch to fit two people walking side by side.

I couldn't help but wonder what this building was, but I had too many other mysteries to wonder about to dwell on this one long.

We stopped about halfway along the hallway, where Maura and Orlando's eyes rose to the ceiling. Paranoid, I feared for a moment that they had spotted a snoozing Bloodless… but no, thank God. They were gazing up at a trapdoor.

Orlando removed the hook from his belt and, with perfect aim, threw it up to the ceiling where it connected with a metal loop that was attached to the trapdoor. He pulled downward hard, and the door dropped open. Then Orlando dropped to his knees and Maura climbed onto his shoulders before he stood again on slightly unsteady feet. She reached up into the hole in the ceiling and grabbed hold of something. A sliding ladder. She drew it down to the ground as Orlando lowered to his knees with her. Removing herself from his shoulders, Maura steadied the ladder on the floor and then began climbing up.

Once she was halfway up the ladder, Orlando gestured for me to follow, which I did eagerly. The thought of escaping to somewhere safe—however dark or damp or cramped it might be—was incredibly appealing to me. As long as it was dry and Bloodless-free, I would find relief there.

Indeed, the loft I entered as I reached the top of the ladder was both of these things. It was also a much nicer-looking loft than the one I had woken up in some hours ago. Well, *nice* might be too strong a word for it, but it was certainly more comfortable-looking. More homely. There were twin mattresses on either side of the room. Both of them looked thicker, with warmer blankets and fluffier pillows. And there was a greater array of paraphernalia here in general. Everything was also neater, cleaner and more organized. A large chest of drawers was nestled in one corner, and there was a table with two chairs. There was also a skylight here, with a rickety ladder leading up to it. Beneath the table were stacks of canned food, along with large bottles of water. I counted in total six gas lamps, positioned around the large room. On the wall opposite of the table was a narrow door that I guessed may have led to a bathroom. I realized only now how full my bladder was—but I was too distracted to pay attention to my need to pee just now. Too many questions were boiling up within me, and as Orlando closed the trap door and bolted it firmly shut, now was the time for me to get some answers.

"Who are you?" I asked.

Maura and Orlando took their time in answering. Orlando set the blade-wheel down in one corner. They both removed their masks again and placed them on the table. Then they removed their jackets and headed to the narrow door. As they stepped inside it, the lamp light revealed that it was indeed a bathroom. It held a toilet, a small sink, and a shower. *Is there running water in this place?* If there was no electricity, I didn't understand why there would be running water.

Orlando and Maura pulled off their soiled pants, stripping to their underwear and dumping the pants in the bathtub. They did the same with their jackets, socks and tops, until they wore nothing but their underwear. With such an extensive view of their bodies, I could see just how emaciated they looked. It really was a wonder they were able to pull off the stunts they did.

Finally, they removed their gloves. My eyes bulged as I caught sight of their hands. Of their fingers. They… they had no fingernails.

"Guys," I said, my breathing quickening. "Please, give me some answers. Who are you? Are you the ones who saved me from the river and put me up in that old loft? Please, answer me."

Maura scowled as she glanced at her pale self in the slightly discolored bathroom mirror. "Just put her out of her misery, will you, Orlando?" she muttered.

Orlando exited the bathroom and first headed to the cabinet, which he drew open. He pulled out some fresh clothes—clean navy blue pants and a baggy t-shirt—before deigning to answer me while he dressed.

"I assume that you have picked up on our names by now," he said, eyeing me furtively. "I am Orlando, and this is my younger sister, Maura."

"Good to meet you," I said, heaving an internal sigh of relief that he was finally beginning an explanation. "I'm Grace," I offered. I would've moved forward to hold out a hand for him to shake, but he had turned his back on me again and was continuing to fish through the cabinet. "Thank you for not leaving me down in that drain and for bringing me with you."

"And as for your other question," Orlando went on, selecting a sweater and pulling it over himself, "yes, it was the two of us who found you in the river and took you up to our old place."

"Your old place?"

"Yes." He sighed, and took a seat in one of the chairs. "We used to live in that loft before we managed to set up in this more secure one."

"Why did you save me?" I asked.

He shrugged, nonchalant. He reached down beneath the table and grabbed a bottle of water before twisting open its lid and taking a swig. "Honestly, it was an accident really. You bumped right into our boat."

"A boat?"

"You clearly need to explain everything to her." Maura

spoke up from the bathroom. "She's obviously not from these parts."

Orlando leaned backward in his seat. He settled his left foot—also nailless—over his right knee and began to massage it absentmindedly as he replied, "We go fishing in that river from time to time for useful objects. You'd be surprised at the type of things people on that side of the river throw away… Something hit against the base of our boat. We thought that we might have collided with some kind of furniture or something. Turns out it was you. Since we had already hauled you out of the river, we figured we ought to help you. We thought that you were human at first—but we couldn't be sure, of course. We managed to break off the handcuffs, and then decided to put you up in our old loft where we could observe you for a while, to see whether you were safe or not… Maura was the one who dried you," he added.

I glanced at Maura with renewed appreciation. "Thank you," I said to her. She kept her back to me as she stood in front of the sink in the bathroom and didn't acknowledge my words. "So you were watching over me?" I directed my question at Orlando.

He nodded. "We were waiting for you to regain

consciousness to see what you would do. We were hanging out on the lower floor for a while."

I thought back to the shadow that had spooked me in the doorway, soon after I had left the loft. Had that been them, watching me silently? I had peeked into that room but, truth be told, I had been too scared to search it thoroughly. It was possible that they had ducked behind some desks, and I had missed spotting them as I had scanned the room.

"Then you decided to wander around," Orlando continued, "and we followed you. When you headed right for the basement and got yourself into such a mess, it was immediately obvious that you were—are—clueless, and so probably also harmless... which was the only reason we followed you down into that drain to help you."

"I'm still wondering if that was a mistake," Maura added. "You had better hope that you don't turn."

I swallowed hard at her words. *Yeah. You and me both, girl.*

"How did you transport me from the river up to that loft?" I asked.

"We couldn't glide with you unconscious, so we had to travel by foot," Orlando explained. "We had to use our wheel to slay a bunch of Bloodless on the way. You're very lucky that we didn't come across any large groups. If we had, we would've abandoned you to save our skin."

I flinched at the blunt honesty of this young man. Though, in a way, it was refreshing. I was a complete and utter stranger to them—obviously, their lives were more valuable to them than mine. Who wouldn't abandon a stranger whom you owed nothing to, if it meant saving your life? Maybe some valiant residents of The Shade, but not ordinary people.

Maura stepped out of the bathroom and set her focus on me. "Who are you, and where did you come from? Why were you in handcuffs? Are you a criminal?"

"I'm not a criminal," I replied. *Though that would depend on who you asked. The IBSI would certainly brand me as one.* "I am a Novak, from The Shade. Have you heard of it?"

They both looked at me blankly. "The Shade? What's that?"

"It's an island in the Pacific Ocean—home to a myriad of supernaturals and humans. Though it's invisible, and only those with express permission are able to enter."

"Never heard of it," Orlando said.

It was strange to think that there were still folks who didn't know about The Shade. Over the years, more and more people had found out about it—I'd thought that its existence had pretty much infiltrated public consciousness by now.

"Where exactly are you from, then?" I asked.

"Manhattan," Orlando replied.

Manhattan. That was where my mom was from.

"You might as well say jail," Maura added with a bitter smile, as she took a seat next to her brother.

I raised my brows. "Jail?"

"Yes," Maura replied. "We were in jail before we got brought… here."

"Why were you in jail? *Who* brought you here?"

"Start at the beginning, Orlando," Maura muttered as she stooped for a can of lentils and cracked it open.

"All right, well…" Orlando began. "The side of Manhattan where we come from is a hellhole—or at least it was the last time we were free to roam the streets. Which was, I guess, over a year ago now. We were living with our dad, since our mom passed away when we were kids. But then one night he disappeared… God knows what happened to him." His eyes glazed over at the memory. He fell silent and somber for several moments before continuing. "After he was gone, we were left to fend for ourselves. And, well…" Here, he shifted uncomfortably in his seat. "I'm not gonna sugarcoat it. We resorted to theft. It was the fastest, easiest way to put food in our stomachs twice a day… at least until we got caught and locked away."

"Jobs aren't exactly abundant where we come from," Maura added darkly. "Not that that's an excuse for stealing, I guess… But if you've stolen once, it's all too easy to do it again."

It was hard to tell from the siblings' expressions whether they were remorseful or not. The way they recounted the story was matter-of-fact, without a lot of emotion inserted into it.

"Anyway," Orlando continued. "We did a bunch of short terms in jail, since we weren't about to give up the habit. But then we got into a crapload of trouble. We underestimated one old grocery store keeper…"

"Almost blew our heads off," Maura said, grimacing.

They both fell silent.

"And?" I prompted.

Their gazes shifted uncomfortably to each other before

Orlando confessed, "Well, we ended up committing manslaughter."

I gulped.

Who have I gotten myself holed up with?

These siblings are murderers.

Orlando cleared his throat. "We got caught again. This time, obviously, we were in much hotter water... Ended up getting the death penalty, the two of us."

"Death penalty?" I asked. Though I shouldn't have been surprised. The government was so low on resources due to various supernatural crises that they now sentenced people to quick execution for all kinds of crimes.

Orlando nodded.

"So, uh, how did you end up here?" I pressed.

"It all started on a Tuesday, if I remember right," Orlando replied.

"It was a Tuesday," Maura confirmed, leaning back in her chair and stretching out her arms and legs.

"A Tuesday. But we can't say how long ago," Orlando went on. "I'm guessing several months. It's funny how I remember it like it was yesterday, though. I was in my cell, lying on my back and staring up at the ceiling. It was two days before Maura's and my execution... along with a dozen or so other inmates'. Two men came to the door of my cell that Tuesday morning—one Caucasian, one African-American. Both wore black from head to foot. They told me that they were from an organization called the IBSI... International Bureau for Supernatural Investigation, I think is what it stands for. They said they had come to make me an offer. They said that they were test-driving a new type of drug, though they refused to give details about what it was exactly. They just said that it was for a good cause, and it could potentially affect the lives of millions of people. They had apparently made some deal with the government, giving those criminals sentenced to death 'a second chance to be of use to society'... 'a second life', or whatever..."

Orlando rose to his feet, and began pacing up and down the room. "Well, you can guess what option I chose. Wasn't exactly a difficult decision. I didn't know what the drug trial would involve, but I had no other options on the table. Anything seemed better than death, at the time. Besides, they told me that I would be able to reunite with my sister, too, since she had already accepted the offer. Right, Maura?"

"Yup." Maura nodded grimly.

"So I left my cell with those two guys that very hour," Orlando said. "They handcuffed me, along with about a dozen other men in my part of the jail, who were also due to be executed. We were taken to a large black truck. We were bundled inside and locked up, along with a bunch of other female convicts, including Maura.

"There were no windows in the back of the vehicle, so we couldn't see where we were being taken. But after a few hours, the vehicle stopped and two men opened up the back. They stepped inside, both of them holding a bunch of needles. They said that they needed to inject us with something for the purpose of 'preparation.' They gave us no choice about it. They moved from one of us to the other, sinking syringes into our arms.

"Soon after that, I lost consciousness. And when I woke again, I was lying flat on my stomach in the middle of a road. A cold, hard, road. It was raining buckets, and when my vision cleared enough, I realized that I was surrounded by buildings, in some urban area. And I wasn't alone. Surrounding me were most of the other men I'd been taken into the truck with, as well as the women. I spotted Maura, lying down also, looking..." He gulped. "Pale. Really pale. I didn't know where I was, where we had been taken, or why we had just been dumped in the middle of a road in the pouring rain. We only realized later that we were in old Chicago."

"Orlando managed to rouse me." Maura continued the story. "And bit by bit, we pieced together our whereabouts. Though to this day, we've never found out why we were dumped here." She glanced down at her pale, nailless hands. "And we've never understood what they did to us exactly."

"We just assumed that the drug experiment—whatever it was—had gone wrong, and they'd dumped us out on the street to rot. Confusing, right?" Orlando said, raising his brows at me.

"Y-Yes," I stammered. My mind was buzzing as I tried to process everything they were telling me. "Can you just confirm one thing for me? You were definitely humans before they took you, right?"

The siblings nodded.

Right.

"They left us with no note or explanation after they dumped us here," Orlando ploughed on, "and none of the other convicts understood what had happened either. None of us had been conscious during whatever procedure we had undergone. But all of us were just thankful that we had apparently been set free—"

"Until we realized that they had given us the equivalent of a death sentence... just longer and more painful," Maura added in a low voice.

"Meaning?" I asked.

Both of them fell silent. Orlando placed his hands down on the table, his head tilted downward, his back facing me. Maura set her can of lentils aside, looking quite sick.

"Whatever procedure they carried out on us," Orlando said finally, his voice becoming husky, "is fatal."

I hesitated before asking, "How do you know that?"

"Because we've seen it," Orlando said, turning around and facing me. In spite of his stoic expression, I couldn't miss the flash of fear in his deep-set eyes. "We've seen it in others. Others who underwent the IBSI's procedure and were thrust out here. Others whose systems were messed up and who turned into... whatever the hell we are. We've watched people die from the effect these changes had on their bodies."

"And people just... disappear," Maura added in a soft voice. "I guess some get caught and turned by the Bloodless, leaving them basically unrecognizable. But there's a colossal crematorium near the shore. Once in a while, tanks sweep through the city—clearing the roads, we assume. Not sure why they even bother." Maura's voice trailed off while she continued to gaze down at her fingers. It was as though she was speaking to herself more than anyone else as she continued, "They say it creeps up on you. They say one day your organs just collapse in on themselves with barely any warning… although they also say that coughing up blood is one of the first symptoms of the body surrendering to its fate." She reached into the pocket of the jogging pants she had changed into and withdrew a pale handkerchief. She twisted it in her fingers absentmindedly. "I fear the day this will be stained with red."

My mouth had completely dried out by now, my mind filled with thoughts of Lawrence. I found myself replaying all the time that we had spent together—recalling every symptom he had ever displayed. I recalled when he had been lying in his hospital bed… He had coughed up blood.

Although Lawrence had still had fingernails, his hair was thin, like Maura and Orlando's. And his skin, as I had already noted, had been thin and pale like theirs.

And his temperature… I realized that I had not felt how cold they were yet. When Orlando had touched me before, he had been wearing gloves.

"Are you cold?" I asked.

Maura slid a hand across the table, allowing me to touch it. Yes, she was cold. But not cold enough to be a full-fledged vampire. Her temperature was about the same as Lawrence's had been.

I believed without any doubt now that whatever procedure the IBSI had inflicted on these siblings—along with God knew how many other human test subjects— was the same type that Lawrence had undergone. Yes, Lawrence's symptoms had not been exactly the same as Orlando and Maura's, but there could be a number of explanations for that. For one, it could be that by the time Lawrence was subjected to the procedure, more time had passed and the IBSI's "test" had developed further, morphed and advanced.

Atticus, when he had come to The Shade to reclaim Lawrence from us, had told us that the procedure was performed to enhance a human's capabilities beyond what had ever been achieved before. But I had no idea whether that was true or not. I couldn't believe a word that man spoke.

Atticus had also claimed that Lawrence had been a half-blood before the procedure—that he had been half-turned by a hungry vampire. But now I didn't believe that either. Orlando and Maura had confirmed that they had been human—and it was the procedure that had caused them to become like this...

The same had to be true for Lawrence.

I thought back to when I had been taken before Atticus in their Chicago headquarters and spoken to him via the screen. I had asked how Lawrence was. Atticus had said that Lawrence had recovered and was doing very well.

What did that mean? Even if he had been telling the truth, *what* exactly would Lawrence be now? What would he have morphed into, if the procedure had been successful?

I brought my mind back to the present. Coughing my dry throat clear, I asked, "So are there many more still living like you? How many, uh, non-Bloodless are there around this side of the city?"

"Impossible for us to give a meaningful estimate," Orlando replied. "But trust me, you don't want to go venturing into the streets out to find out. In case you hadn't picked up on it already, Maura and I try to keep to ourselves as much as possible."

"Some of the other 'humans'," Maura explained, forming air quotes with her fingers, "if we can call ourselves that, can be more vicious and desperate than the Bloodless."

"What do you mean?" I asked.

"For one thing," Orlando replied, "they're all thugs. Violent convicts, most with a lot fewer scruples than us. Add to that the fact that they are in dire, desperate circumstances, struggling to survive in this hellhole— they're utterly ruthless. They've formed into gangs. They roam the buildings and roads, preying on those weaker than them... not all that dissimilar to the Bloodless themselves. And if any suspect you have food or shelter that's better than theirs, they'll hunt you down and..."

"Make you wish you were dead, basically," Maura finished, her lips forming a hard line.

"D-Did they ever hunt you?" I asked, shaken. This place truly was the stuff of nightmares.

"It happened to us once," Maura said. "A month or so ago. It was early evening. We had been foraging for food, and we got spotted and mugged—everything we'd spent the day collecting stripped from us… We were just lucky we managed to get away and lose them before they could follow us. Since then, we've been out far less."

"Have you ever tried to escape from here?" I asked. "Find somewhere safer, like on the other side of the river?"

"Oh, trust me, we have tried," Orlando scoffed. "That was one of the first things we figured that we ought to do when we found ourselves in this place. Well, we were sure in for a rude awakening. There are guards with guns keeping watch on that side of the river for anyone attempting to cross the boundary—which is, by the way, electrified anyway." Orlando's right hand hovered over his right hip. "We both got bullets lodged in us before we could even reach the fence. I got two, by my hip. Maura got one in her arm. It's amazing that the two of us survived it. It's like our bodies have toughened in some way… Obviously, we never tried again after that." Orlando grimaced. "We might have a fatal condition, but suicide has never been the way I want to go."

"Me neither," Maura said. She picked up her tin of lentils again and continued eating slowly.

I stared at the siblings, at their macabre expressions. From the way they spoke so plainly about their pending demise, it was clear that they'd known for a long time now that they would die young. After all, they had been sentenced to execution. I supposed that they saw this extra extension of their life provided by the IBSI—however grim an existence it was—as time they would never have had anyway.

As our conversation fell into a natural lull, the three of us falling into our own thoughts, I realized that I couldn't wait any longer to relieve myself. I asked to use the bathroom, and locked myself inside. After emptying my bladder, I pulled the flush absentmindedly, and to my surprise, it actually did flush. There was running water. I moved to the sink and turned on the tap. More running water.

I couldn't help but find that strange. How long had this part of Chicago been like this? It must have been years. And yet the authorities continued to provide a water supply. It seemed almost like a courtesy to those living here, to not leave them completely abandoned. But courtesy was not something that I linked with the IBSI.

Shaking away the thoughts, I dried my hands and returned to the main room. Maura had finished her lentils and moved to one of the mattresses, where she lay on her side, facing the wall, her back turned to the rest of the loft. Orlando was seated again at the table, tucking into his own tin of lentils.

As I sat down next to him, he gestured to the supply of tinned food beneath the table. "Are you hungry?" he asked.

I shook my head. I was many things right now, but hungry definitely wasn't one of them.

"So," Orlando said, brushing the side of his mouth with the back of his hand, "are you going to tell us how exactly you got here? Why were you in handcuffs, if you aren't a criminal?"

I paused, still mulling over everything the siblings had told me until now. I really wasn't in the mood to start talking about myself, but it was only courteous to respond in kind. "I came across something that the IBSI really wants to keep secret… FOEBA."

Orlando's long face scrunched up in confusion. "What's that? Sounds like some kind of infection."

I heaved a sigh. "Well, that's just it. I was roaming around IBSI's headquarters back in Hawaii, trying to get some clues. I had managed to infiltrate it, but then I got caught and taken to Chicago. I was unable to uncover anything at all other than the fact it's something the IBSI is extremely touchy about." I explained to him in brief about the thumb drive Arwen and I had found. As I thought of Arwen, I felt a sharp pang in my chest. Where was she now? Where were my parents? Were they still on the mission in the ogres' realm with the League? Did they know that I was missing yet?

Thinking about the stress my family would be in once they found out I was gone tied my stomach up in knots.

I had to find a way to get back to them.

I cut my explanation short and turned my focus on the main obstacle facing me: reaching a phone.

"Orlando," I said, "Do you have any—"

"I'm going to sleep now," Maura called irritably from her corner, interrupting me. "So if you're gonna keep talking, keep your tone down, please."

"Sorry," I murmured, glancing at her before returning my attention to Orlando.

He finished the last of his lentils and stood up. "It's best we don't talk here then," he said. "Come with me."

Maura sat up. "Where are you going?" she asked her brother. Anxiety showed in her eyes as she clutched her blanket.

"It's okay, Maura," he said. "We'll just climb up to the

roof and sit there a bit."

"Go via the skylight, so you can hear me if I call," she said. The angst in her voice reminded me of a child who was afraid of the dark. Quite at odds with the tough exterior she'd put on around me until now. I looked at her curiously as she settled back down on her mattress and pulled up her blanket. Clearly, there were layers of these two siblings that I had yet to unravel.

Orlando gripped the ladder, checking that it was steady, before he began to climb it. When he reached the glass in the ceiling, he fiddled with the latch and then pushed upward, easing it open. Splashes of rainwater trickled down into the loft as he slid out.

He gazed down at me. "Are you coming or not?"

The truth was, I would so much rather stay down here in the dry warmth. The last thing I wanted to do was go outside again, but, taking hold of the ladder, I climbed up to him and joined him in standing on the roof. At least the rain was not as intense as it had been. It was more of a light drizzle now—still unpleasant and chilling, though.

"Oh, hey," I said, "Do you have a lighter, or matches?"

"I have a lighter," he said, dipping into his pocket and handing one to me. I ignited a flame and coaxed it into my palms. I cradled it and balled it into a larger fire to keep the two of us warm as we sat and gazed out at the gray city sprawled around us.

Orlando stared at the flames in my hands. "Do you have any other powers?" he asked.

"I can mess with water," I replied, "and sometimes I can manipulate wind, too." The latter, admittedly, I wasn't very practiced at, but I'd noticed since I was young that I could redirect gusts of wind, or cause them to be stronger to a certain degree.

Orlando's almost-black eyes lingered on my face. "Maybe you won't turn, after all," he commented.

Thanks for reminding me.

I glanced down at my legs. The stinging of the puncture wounds was definitely less than before, and had not been replaced with some other kind of excruciating pain. Maybe Orlando was right. I had heard that Bloodless did not affect everyone—for example, according to Aisha, they couldn't turn witches. Or werewolves, or other supernatural species that weren't vampires. Maybe the fae blood running in me was just enough to stop me from turning as a normal human would.

I let out a long, slow breath, allowing myself to

experience a moment of relief—a feeling that had become practically foreign to me in the past few days. The relief might have been unfounded—since, as Maura had pointed out, it could also simply be that the turning process was delayed due to me being half-human. But for now, I let it wash over me. There was only so much stress a person could take before they snapped.

And there was no point in worrying about something that might or might not happen—something that I had absolutely no control over right now. I had to simply do what I could… and that brought me right back to the subject I needed to ask Orlando about right now: *How do I find a phone?*

"I need to make contact with my people, back in The Shade," I said. "Do you have any idea where I might find a working phone?"

"A working phone," Orlando repeated. His blank expression immediately made my heart sink to my stomach. "There are plenty of broken phones around here, but you won't find any working ones. That was something that Maura and I tried to locate in the beginning. We have an uncle in New York whom we wanted to contact to inform him about what had happened to us… and ask whether there was something he might be able to do to help. Let's just say we failed miserably."

"What about in the neighboring human settlements?" I asked him. "I know you said that trying to gain entrance to the civilization on the other side of the river—where the IBSI is keeping watch—is pointless and dangerous. But there must be some other normal, human civilization somewhere nearby. What about further east? What about on the other side of Lake Michigan? You already have a boat, don't you? What if we followed the river and just... sailed away from this pit?"

Orlando pursed his lips, his eyes fixed on the grim skyline.

"It's a nice idea," he said simply.

"Well?" I pressed, frustrated.

"Boat is rather a flattering term for what Maura and I were floating in when we found you," he replied. "It's just a raft made of junk."

"So you've never tried to reach the coast? Have you ever searched for a proper boat? I can't believe there's not a single vessel on the shore that doesn't have some kind of communication device. Even if the signal is out in this whole area, we could travel to somewhere that does have a working signal and—"

Orlando shook his head, cutting me off. "That part of the city is notorious for the most brutal gangs. It's also where the Bloodless are most concentrated. The odds of you even reaching the shore alive are low… If the Bloodless don't get to you first, the criminals will."

"But if you've never been there, how do you—"

"We know," he said, impatient, "because we've been told. Although we do lock ourselves up and try to avoid everyone, there are a handful of other survivors whom we are on semi-decent terms with. On the few occasions that we happen to pass each other, we exchange information." He exhaled. "Even leaving aside the Bloodless and the criminals, there are electrified fences closing off the shore from the mainland, and there are barriers blocking the river's entry to the lake. One thing the IBSI has made amply obvious to all residents of this craphole is that they want us to stay put… If you don't believe me, go ahead and try it. Try to escape yourself."

I clenched my jaw. Going out again all alone was my very, very last resort. Maura and Orlando knew this city a hundred times better than I did. They knew all its perils, how to dodge them and what to look out for. I was much more likely to survive and be successful with their help. Besides, venturing out alone into this place of nightmares… I gulped. It was downright terrifying.

In spite of Orlando's words, I still couldn't bring myself to believe that, together, it would be impossible to reach the shore. There *had* to be some way to slip through and find a proper boat. The siblings had their spinning blade-wheel thing, and I had my ability to control fire. Joining forces, surely we could pull it off—or at least attempt it without losing our lives.

I voiced my thoughts to Orlando, and in the end, he agreed with me that it *might* be possible, but… there wasn't an ounce of life or enthusiasm in him to attempt it, even with my help. Maybe he really was just past thinking he could escape this place. Maybe they had just had one too many failed escape attempts and were worn out, preferring to accept this as their life. Since they had already accepted that they were going to die from the IBSI's treatment, maybe, in their last days or weeks—who knew how long they had left to live—they simply wanted to avoid trouble as much as possible. Retreat into their shells.

That would definitely be consistent with Maura's behavior—her desire to just leave me in that sewage tunnel… though I could not deny that they had gone to the trouble of chasing after me in the first place and rescuing me. Then Orlando had insisted that they bring me with them. They definitely had *some* fire left in them.

Maybe the problem was that they just didn't know where they would be escaping *to* anymore. Maybe they thought that, even if they managed to escape, they would simply be recaptured again. After all, outside this Bloodless territory, the siblings were practically as good as dead anyway, having been sentenced to execution by the government. They would have to spend the rest of however long their lives were in hiding… on the run… which was basically how they lived now.

But what if I could make them see something more for their future? What if…

"What if we tried to escape, and find a boat, and together look for a phone?" I said, breaking the silence. "And what if I made you a promise that, if we found a phone, I would bring you back to The Shade? Our safe, beautiful island where there is no shortage of food or amenities. Even if you're convinced that you're going to die, I assure you that your last days will be better spent on our island than here."

I realized as I said the words that I was promising a place on our island to convicted murderers. But my brain was muddled with desperation right now. I *had* to get back home. Besides, at least from what they had told me, they had murdered because they had been lacking food. If we provided them with everything they needed, I didn't see a reason why they couldn't be like normal upstanding citizens…

But I was getting ahead of myself. *Way* ahead of myself.

I widened my eyes at Orlando, waiting for his response.

"Even if we managed to escape, and even if we found a working phone and managed to contact your people back in *The Shade*," he mused, "what makes you think that we would be welcome?"

"My grandparents are king and queen," I replied proudly. "My parents are prince and princess. I would find a way for you to stay. That really ought to be the least of your worries."

He rubbed his face in his palms and went quiet for several minutes. When he raised his head again and met my eyes, his expression was dark, but set with resolution.

"All right, Grace," he said in a low voice. "I'll talk to Maura in the morning. If she agrees, we'll try it."

"Not try." I imagined the oracle's words in my head, the way my father told me she had once spoken to him. *"Trying is for cowards."*

I set my jaw in determination and gave Orlando a hard stare. "If she agrees," I corrected him, "we will do it."

He coughed out a dry laugh. "A lot easier said than done, Grace," he muttered grimly. "A *lot* easier said than done…"

Chapter 5: Ben

After we had recovered the ogre king, Anselm Raskid, and his people from the hunters' clutches in their hideout beneath the lake, the League continued to search for other IBSI bases that might've sprung up around The Trunchlands. We found several others and destroyed them all before obliterating the final one—the one closest to the gate leading back to the human realm, which had been the one that had alerted us to the IBSI's presence in The Trunchlands to begin with.

Then we decided to return to The Shade. We had to consider carefully what our next move ought to be. If we had discovered the IBSI's footprints in The Woodlands and The Trunchlands, there was a good possibility that they had already set up in other realms too. I found myself wondering whether The Tavern had been affected yet. To me, that was the obvious place for the League to head next. Even if the IBSI had not made their presence felt there yet, there was a myriad of supernatural creatures passing through it and we should be able to quite easily gain the latest news and rumors of the IBSI's movements.

We returned to Earth via the gate on the ogres' beach. Kyle was waiting patiently with *Nightshade* on the other side. To my aunt Vivienne and uncle Xavier's great dismay, he informed us that Victoria and Bastien had come this way, along with Regan and Azaiah. They had been on their way to the Blackhalls' lair in The Woodlands, he said. After a worried conversation, Xavier decided that he too would head for The Woodlands.

"I'm going to bring Vicky home," Xavier said firmly to Vivienne. "She might be an adult, but I don't care in this case. She's still a teenager and it's a completely unnecessary risk, her hanging out in werewolf territory. Things are simply still too volatile between the dimensions for that right now."

I certainly didn't think that it was a good idea at all that Victoria returned there—even with dragons accompanying her—since there wasn't a speck of supernatural blood in her. She was human and vulnerable. But it seemed that she really had fallen for Bastien. I knew all too well how hard it was to be apart from somebody you loved, even if it meant risking danger.

One of the dragons, Neros, volunteered to go with Xavier—both of them knew where to find the Blackhalls' lair, since we had visited there already during our stay in The Woodlands. The vampire and dragon headed off, back to the supernatural dimension, while the rest of us piled into *Nightshade* to begin the short journey to our island.

I caught my wife's hand as we made our way through the chopper, toward one of the empty back rows. River sat in the window seat and I sat next to her. As the aircraft prepared to take off, she leaned against my shoulder and slid one arm around my midriff. I kissed the top of her head, wrapping my own arm around her and pulling her close.

"You okay?" I asked. We had barely had any time alone recently with all the craziness that had been going on.

"Yeah," she replied softly. "I'm just thinking about Grace... wondering how she's been doing."

"Yeah," I said, leaning my head back against my chair. I gazed down into River's turquoise eyes and we shared a smile.

"I'm so proud of her, you know," River said.

My smile broadened. "I know," I replied, dipping to kiss her lips.

I couldn't have wished for a better daughter than Grace. I saw many of River's qualities in her—her caring nature, her honesty and strength, to name a few—and I also hoped that I had managed to instill in Grace a lesson or two from what I had learned and been taught over my years of living.

I did worry about her though. It would be a lie to say otherwise. As much as The Shade's way of raising children had changed—going from trying to stifle them and keep them away from danger at all costs, to encouraging them to develop the skills and experience to face it—of course, as a parent, I could never stop worrying. Now that I had Grace, I could appreciate more than ever what my parents had been through when Rose and I had been away from The Shade on our misadventures.

It hurt deep inside to watch your child walking into

danger. But this was the world we lived in now. And I hoped that River and I had prepared Grace well for it.

River and I eased into a relaxed silence while we gazed out the window and watched the ground disappear beneath us. I relished the peace, the feel of my love in my arms as we soared back toward The Shade.

I had to admit that after almost two decades of possessing this fae body, my time as a ghost and those harrowing days I'd spent in The Underworld seemed so far off, so distant, almost like a different life. Although I would never, and could never, forget all that had happened, never taking a physical body for granted was still a decision I had to make every day.

But there were some things in life that you just couldn't take for granted, even if you tried… and for me, that was River. She was my soulmate through and through. In all the twenty years we had been married, we'd rarely had arguments. Disagreements, yes, but never bitterness. We understood each other too well for that. We lived in line with one another. As she held my heart completely, I held hers. I'd never really understood the love that my parents shared until I met River. I'd never understood what it was like to feel like you couldn't live without another person—

as if without them, all would be for nothing. And as we had aged mentally over the years, it felt like my attachment to her had only grown stronger. There wasn't a lot that could frighten me anymore, but a life without River was a thought that drove me to the edge.

"We're almost home," River announced, pointing out of the window to a familiar rock formation jutting out of the ocean. She looked up at me, apparently noticing my contemplative mood. "What are you thinking about?" she asked.

I gazed down at her adoringly. Reaching a hand to her face, I brushed my thumb against her cheek.

"That I forgot to remind you about something today," I replied, assuming a serious expression.

She frowned, clearly racking her brain as to what it could be. "What?" she asked.

I caught her lips in mine before replying, "That I love you."

"You're such a cheeseball, Ben." She chuckled against my kiss, even as she draped her arms around my neck and returned it tenderly. Then her voice dropped to a whisper. "But you know I do love cheese…"

We enjoyed the last stretch of the journey together

before my father, who was sitting near the front of the aircraft with my mother, stood and called to everyone, "We'll be landing in a couple of minutes. I know we could all do with some rest, but before we head back to our homes, I'm going to ask you all to attend a meeting in the Dome. We'll keep it brief, I promise, but we need to discuss how long a break to take and start throwing a few ideas around as to our next destination."

I groaned internally. Right now, I wanted nothing more than to go with River to look for Grace. But I understood my father's reasoning. So, after Kyle touched us down in the glade in front of the Black Heights, we all headed to the Great Dome.

We didn't make it that far, however.

An anxious-looking Shayla came hurrying toward us, through the trees along the forest path. She looked like she hadn't slept in days.

"Oh! Thank God you're back!" she exclaimed. To my surprise, she looked past everyone else in the crowd and her eyes settled on River and me. My gut dropped instinctively, even before she said, "Grace is in trouble!"

River's breath hitched.

"What?" River and I spluttered.

My stomach knotted tighter and tighter as Shayla began to tell us how Grace had developed a friendship with the sickly boy, Josh—or rather, Lawrence—and how she had been very disturbed when he left. She hadn't trusted his father who'd come to reclaim him, and she'd wanted to investigate his circumstances. She and Arwen had gone off together to fish for some clues and—*dammit!*—the two girls had gone to Hawaii. Into the IBSI's base. Arwen had told Shayla everything that happened: Grace had not come back out when she'd been expected to, and while Arwen had been waiting, she'd met with some trouble on the beach—a crowd of hunters who'd been patrolling had managed to detect her, which caused her to become distracted from monitoring the tracker for a short while as she tried to find a safe spot to wait. When she checked the tracker again, Grace's signal wasn't emitting from where it should have been. It was too far away. Over the ocean.

"Arwen says Grace must have been caught and taken somewhere by aircraft," Shayla continued to explain. "Arwen left the beach to try to pinpoint the location, but then the signal vanished completely."

I felt like throwing up.

"Where is my daughter now?" Corrine demanded, her

voice boiling with anger. She wouldn't have known about any of this. After Lucas' discovery of the French girl and her infant in ogres' royal palace, Corrine had left our group to transport the mother and child to The Shade. But she'd stayed on the island only long enough to settle them into the hospital, before rejoining the League.

"She was feeling so awful about it," Shayla replied, "she's gone off with a bunch of other witches to try to track Grace down. The idea was for them to go to the approximate area where Arwen lost Grace's signal and try to figure out which direction she could've gone in. Arwen suspected, though, that they were headed to North America. They took one of the phones, but I haven't yet heard from them since they left, so I don't know how they've been doing or if they've made any progress. But they also took a tracker with them, so you can locate them." Shayla reached into her pocket and handed Corrine a receiving device.

River's panicked gaze met mine. *North America.* Why would they want Grace in North America? *Or, if the tracker has been destroyed, maybe she hasn't even made it that far… No. No.* I shook away the thought violently. I could not start considering the possibility.

"I have to leave," I said, my tone unsteady.

"Where to?" River asked desperately.

I had already started to rise into the air, preparing to begin hurtling across the ocean. "To scour every single IBSI base in the United States if I have to."

"Ben," Lucas spoke up, moving to me. He placed a hand on my shoulder and gave me a hard stare. "This is a mission for supernaturals the hunters aren't yet able to detect—for fae. But more than one would be useful… I'll come with you."

I looked gratefully at my uncle. His support meant the world to me in this moment.

"And I will come too," Kailyn offered.

I glanced from Lucas to her and nodded. My throat was so tight, I could barely even speak to thank them. I glanced over at my family, who all still looked in a state of shock at the news, before my eyes lingered on River. She looked like she wanted to come with me—of course she did—but as my uncle had rightly said, this was a job for fae. Vampires would be more than useless, they would be a hindrance. Even witches would barely be helpful since the hunters' alarm system was able to pick them up.

"Oh, don't think you're leaving me behind," Corrine

seethed. "I've got a thing or two to say to *my* daughter. I'll come with you just as far as her, if you really think you should pull off the rest of the mission alone."

Before leaving with the others, I stooped down quickly to River and grabbed her shoulders. I pulled her to me, giving her one last hug and pressing a firm kiss against her forehead.

"I will find our daughter," I breathed into her hair, "and I will bring her back. I promise."

Chapter 6: River

Grace's disappearance was a horrible form of déjà vu for me. I remembered the time when I had been captured by the hunters all too well. It cut me to the core to imagine what they might be doing to her now. What they might be taking from her. *Whether she's still alive.*

Tears welled in the corners of my eyes as I watched my husband leave with Lucas, Kailyn and Corrine.

But I had to have faith in Ben's words. I had to trust that he would find her— just as he had managed to find me against all odds—and bring her back to safety.

The meeting was held as planned, but it was a sheer

waste of time. None of us Novaks could concentrate on anything, and we all just wanted it to be over. So we wrapped up quickly and I was free to leave. I didn't think I had it in me to concentrate on anything until my husband was safely back home with my daughter.

On leaving the Great Dome, Rose and Sofia hugged me, trying to offer words of comfort. But I could draw none from them. My first instinct now was to go to my mother. She knew exactly what it was like to lose a child, and in this moment, there was nothing that I wanted more than to feel her arms around me.

My heart hammering in my chest, I sped through the redwood trees to the apartment that she shared with my two younger sisters.

On arriving, my sisters were out, but my mom was home. Her face lit up to see me, but then dropped instantly on noticing my expression. She pulled me inside, and I told her everything that had happened. Even though I trusted my husband, I couldn't hold back the tears. This was the first time I'd ever experienced losing Grace. She had spent her whole life on the island, and since the day she was born, I'd always known where she was—that she was safe somewhere within its borders. Even more recently, when she'd started going out on missions with the League, Ben and I had always been there to keep a close eye on her. This was a brand-new emotion that I was experiencing, and it felt like somebody had bored a hole in my heart.

I sat with my mother for a while in her living room, trying to calm my nerves and stop my mind from playing over all the worst possible scenarios. Then my mother suggested that we go out for a walk and get some fresh air, which I eagerly agreed to. We left her penthouse and strolled through the woods, heading for the beach.

"Grace is a tough one," my mother said as we removed our shoes and dipped our feet in the waves. "And she is a lot less vulnerable than you were."

My mother held my hand and continued trying to keep my mood up while we walked, keep me thinking positively... and I tried. I truly tried.

After about an hour of breathing in the fresh ocean air, I couldn't deny that I was feeling a tad calmer—the seeming infinity of the water surrounding our island often had a way of doing that to me—but my stomach was still aching.

We turned around and decided to head back. We lapsed

into silence and I fixed my eyes on the sky, remembering how, not far from here, I had once prayed for Ben to find his way back to me. That was when I'd thought that I had lost him forever after discovering he was a ghost. He had appeared behind me soon after, and it had seemed like a miracle at the time. I wasn't exactly expecting that to happen now, but then… something so entirely unexpected happened that I thought I must've been hallucinating.

A streak of black hurtling across the sky above The Shade's boundary caught my eye. Then I lost sight of it just as quickly as it had appeared. It had looked far too large to be a bird, and yet it definitely hadn't been an aircraft either.

I felt a bit crazy just thinking of it, but it had looked like… some other kind of flying animal. I was sure that it had four legs. But now, as I gazed around trying to spot it again, I couldn't find it for the life of me. There wasn't a single trace of it having been anything other than a figment of my imagination. *Maybe Grace's absence literally is making me insane.*

"You all right, honey?" my mother asked, noticing me looking around with a confused expression on my face. "What are you looking for?"

I didn't answer for several moments as I continued to scan the heavens. When I still didn't spy it again, I could only conclude, "It was nothing."

Chapter 7: Victoria

Spending time with Bastien in his castle was like a dream. A fairytale, almost. I felt as if I was floating on clouds, and I wasn't sure that I would ever come down. Although much of his time during the day was occupied by coming to grips with his responsibilities as the new ruler of the Blackhalls, I was just so overjoyed to be with him.

It was also incredibly interesting to witness the ins and outs of a werewolf chieftain's duties. I supposed I had never really thought much about it, but they functioned much like any ruler would, including those in The

Shade. All ultimate decisions lay with him. The emphasis on food and defense seemed to be the greatest. He had to ensure there were enough food scavengers bringing in a constant supply for the pack, and ensure their territory was properly guarded.

Even though I wasn't a wolf, the fact that everyone saw me as Bastien's "girlfriend"—a term that Bastien had to clarify for the others, as I had once clarified for him—meant that I was treated with the same respect as Bastien. I felt pretty awkward about it all, considering that I was basically just Bastien's shadow. I wanted to contribute, and help wherever I could, but so far there wasn't an awful lot that I could do—since Bastien himself was still learning the ropes, with the help of his elderly friend and advisor, Cecil.

All the while, Azaiah and Regan were kind enough to stay with me. Though they didn't end up spending that much time in the castle. They seemed to enjoy themselves going out to roam the Woodlands—scaring hundreds of wolves in the process, I was sure. But I trusted the two of them to not give into the temptation of scooping up a wolf for a snack. They were content with other eatables they found around this place.

One good piece of news was that, after the upheaval that had so recently taken place in The Woodlands, the wolves had been forced to work together. Tensions between many of the tribes seemed to have reduced. Several chieftains came to visit Bastien after learning of his appointment, seeking to form alliances with the Blackhalls.

Cecil also suggested that Bastien ought to make some trips of his own, to reach out to some other chieftains to introduce himself as the new Blackhall leader, and start a dialogue with them... the Bonereavers, however, were definitely not on that list. Cecil advised that Bastien go with ten other wolves from the pack while the recent hunter invasion was still fresh in the minds of the wolves of The Woodlands. Bastien began to make plans to leave, discussing details with his council. He approached me last. I had already anticipated the reluctance in his expression before I witnessed it.

He didn't want me to go traveling across The Woodlands again, of course. And I accepted that. It was pushing it just for me to be here in his castle to begin with.

I resigned myself to the fact that my stay would only

last a few more days, until Bastien and his companions departed on their journey. He wasn't sure how long they would be gone. I didn't know when I might be able to visit him again. He said to be safe, I ought not return for at least a week and a half. A week and a half wasn't long by normal standards, but I was already imagining how slowly the hours would tick by without him.

I also knew that the time we had left together would go by in a flash, and it seemed he realized it as well. He informed Cecil he would need some more free time until he departed. Cecil agreed to take over some of his duties and slow down on his training, so that we could have more time together.

On the evening Bastien and I had agreed I would depart, he completed his duties in the early evening. I was expecting us to go up to his apartment, where we usually went to get away from everyone. This time, to my surprise, he suggested that we head out for a walk— close to his lair, but far enough for us to stretch our legs a bit. We could feel more alone with each other, in peace and quiet, without the bustle of the pack beneath us.

I hadn't been out of the mountain even once since I arrived, and The Woodlands was an absolutely beautiful place. Twining my fingers with his, I was looking forward to seeing where Bastien was planning to take me. But we didn't make it far. We had barely walked halfway across the grassland in front of the Blackhalls' mountain when I spotted my father. He was marching toward me, his jaw firmly set, a look of determination in his eyes. Behind him was a dragon, Neros. I guessed the League had finished their latest mission and returned to Kyle, who'd informed them of my whereabouts.

My heart sank to my stomach. Bastien and I stopped in our tracks, staring at him. My father reached us in seconds, and, glancing at Bastien briefly, set his focus on me. Somehow, I already knew what he was going to say before he even parted his lips.

"Victoria," he said heavily, "I'm very disappointed that you came back here. You need to come home."

I swallowed hard, my own disappointment clawing at my chest.

My shoulders sagged. "Well, I was planning to come home, anyway, after a few days…" I murmured.

"You need to come home with me, *now*," he said.

I heaved a sigh. There were times when there was no arguing with my father, and I could already tell that this was one of them.

Bastien also looked crestfallen, but he turned to me, clutching both of my hands. "You must go with your father," he said, his soulful gray eyes gazing down into mine.

I faced my father. "Okay, but… I have to visit Bastien again." *Soon.*

I hated the doubt in my father's expression. "Things between the dimensions are very, very turbulent right now, Vicky. We'll talk about that in a week or so."

I couldn't help but feel that even if my parents did sanction my returning for another visit, it wouldn't be nearly as long as this one. I was sure I wouldn't be able to spend a full day, let alone a night… maybe just a few hours.

Bastien seemed to detect my dismay, I guessed because he was experiencing the same fear. He dipped his head and planted a chaste kiss on my lips before giving my hands another squeeze.

"We'll be all right, Victoria," he said quietly.

I nodded, even as I found myself wishing that somebody else had stepped up to take over the Blackhall tribe. But I knew how selfish it was of me to even think such a thing. This was Bastien's place among his people. This was what he was meant to be doing. This was his duty.

"Okay," I said, trying to turn my thoughts around and look on the bright side. The main reason it had been so unbearable the last time I had been separated from Bastien was because of the way we had parted. Him doubting me, and thinking that I might have betrayed him to the hunters. Not knowing whether he'd even survived the IBSI's attack on Rock Hall. Now, the circumstances were totally different. I knew that Bastien was okay here. He had regained his home. And he had people around him—people who respected and appreciated him. He was no longer on his own.

"I should go fetch your dragon friends," Bastien said.

I didn't want to be parted in these last few minutes we had before I left, so I went with him. Unfortunately, the dragons weren't hard to find. They'd been hanging out in one of the lounge rooms on the ground floor, and we found ourselves heading back to the clearing where we'd left my father all too soon.

"I'll give you a moment to say goodbye," my father said to me, his tone softening a little as we returned. He cast another furtive glance at the werewolf before turning around and approaching Neros with Azaiah and Regan. So much had happened, and my parents had been away so much, I hadn't even had a chance to properly talk to them about Bastien yet, to explain how I felt about him. *No doubt now, I will have plenty of time for that*, I thought grimly.

Bastien placed his hands on either side of my neck, his fingers reaching into my hair as he bestowed on me another kiss. A long, deep, mournful kiss.

Bastien's assurance that "we'd be all right" felt too vague. Neither of us could say when we'd see each other again. I was grasping for something more concrete.

"One and a half weeks, you said," I reminded him, "that's when you should be finished on your tour?"

"I hope so," he replied.

"Then I will try to return, then, even if it's just for a few hours. And hopefully, in the coming weeks, some things will change," I went on, though I struggled to understand how they would. "And I'll be able to stay longer with you again. Then you could come to stay in The Shade with me, if you can get some time off."

He smiled at me warmly, brushing his fingers against

my cheek. Then his arms wound around me and he lifted me off my feet in an embrace. "I would love that," he whispered.

"Okay," I said, as he set me back down. I drew in a breath to steady myself. All I wanted was to lose myself in another one of his kisses, keep myself wrapped in his arms a moment longer... but it would only make it harder to pull away.

We took a step away from each other, our bodies parting. I did my best to put on a strong, optimistic face. And so did he.

"Goodbye, Victoria," he said. "I love you."

"Goodbye... I love you too."

I unglued my gaze from him and turned around to make my way toward my father and the dragon. I didn't look back at Bastien until I'd climbed aboard Neros, my father sitting behind me.

Bastien remained rooted to the spot, looking up at me. The breeze caught locks of his curly black hair, making them trail across his handsome face. Even from this distance, his eyes were striking.

I pulled another smile and blew him a kiss. And then, as the dragons took to the air, I watched him grow smaller and smaller on the ground, until a line of trees hid him from my view.

I swallowed.

Okay. This is okay. Bastien and I will just have a long-distance relationship for the time being. Many couples do that and pull through... I comforted myself that we would probably even grow stronger apart, and that the next time we met would be even more special.

"Okay, Vicky?" my father asked behind me, breaking through my thoughts.

"Yeah."

I felt him kiss the back of my head.

We fell into silence as we gazed down at The Woodlands slipping away beneath us. When we reached the shore and launched out over the endless blue, my father cleared his throat and asked, "Do you love him?"

I suspected that he'd wanted to ask that the moment he had gotten me alone.

"Yes," I replied, barely hesitating. *I love that wolf...*

I didn't turn to see my father's reaction, though I felt him tense slightly behind me.

There was another pause before he spoke again,

echoing Bastien's assurance: "Then you'll be all right."

My father couldn't have known how much his words meant to me.

109

CHAPTER 8: BASTIEN

"Goodbye, Victoria," I found myself breathing as I watched her disappear into the sky. My new responsibilities would feel a lot heavier without her presence. My bed would feel a lot colder. I would no longer hear her laughter in the evenings, have her sweet kisses waking me in the mornings. Breathe in her scent as she followed me around during the day. I would be alone now… though, I reminded myself, I was not actually alone. I had Cecil, and a whole pack of wolves who were loyal to me and my family. It would be ungrateful to feel that I was alone. I couldn't take what

I had for granted when only a short while ago I had been without food or shelter, fleeing for not only my life, but my sanity.

Victoria had mentioned to me that her stay in my home had felt like a dream to her, and that was exactly the way it had felt to me too. A dream that had now faded. A dream that I couldn't be sure would ever return.

I had been uncomfortable about Victoria coming to The Woodlands from the very start, as soon as she had proposed the idea. I had given in because... well, she had wanted it, and I had wanted it, too. I had been too selfish, too greedy for her, to hold my ground and insist that she stay in The Shade. Now her father had come to do what I should've done: lead her back to safety.

I tore my eyes away from the empty sky and turned around, heading slowly and heavily back to the castle.

As I reached the entrance, I reminded myself of the assurance I had given Victoria—that we would see each other again. *We will,* I told myself firmly. *Sooner or later, we will.* We had managed to reunite before against all odds. There was no reason why we couldn't now, when the odds were far, far less...

We just had to be patient and wait. I felt a little more

cheerful as I passed through the entrance hall. Victoria was certainly a woman I was willing to wait for.

I had tried to hide it, but those nights she had spent with me in my bed had been torture. More times than I would like to admit, I'd had to fight the urge to claim her as mine... completely. One of my weaknesses was my impulsiveness, the force of my emotions. It was truly a wonder to me that I had managed to control myself and allowed her to leave The Woodlands as she had come— with her virtue intact. In werewolf culture, it wasn't tradition for men and women to share a bed until they had committed themselves to each other in marriage. But with Victoria being a human, her and my relationship had been anything but traditional until now.

"Bastien," Cecil addressed me, spying me in the corridor. "Back so soon? Where is Victoria?"

"She is gone," I said resolutely, "at least for now. Her father came to collect her."

I attempted to turn my mind to other things now— specifically to the journey that lay ahead of me. We could leave sooner now that Victoria was gone.

Traveling would help me take my mind off of her... and hopefully make the days pass more quickly.

Chapter 9: Grace

After Orlando had agreed to talk to his sister about escaping with me to The Shade, we left the roof and returned to the dry loft. Maura appeared to be sleeping by now; her chest heaved gently as she lay beneath her blankets on the mattress. Orlando and I took it in turns to use the bathroom in preparation for bed. He provided me with a pair of snowflake pajamas that were brand-new—still in their plastic packaging. I guessed that they had foraged for these in a store or something downtown. I changed into them and disposed of my old clothes in the trashcan.

There were only two mattresses in the loft, though they had an impressive stock of pillows and blankets in their cupboard. Orlando laid two blankets one on top of the other in a relatively empty corner of the loft. He gave me a third blanket to cover myself with, and a pillow.

I sank into the makeshift bed and turned on my side. I gazed at the tall, sickly Orlando on the opposite end of the room and experienced an uncanny wave of déjà vu as I thought of Lawrence.

Orlando stooped to his mattress and lay down. He turned his back on me, facing the ceiling. I watched through the dim lighting of the one gas lamp he had left on as his breathing grew slower and heavier.

Although my body was completely exhausted, and I needed as much rest as I could get, for the life of me, I couldn't fall asleep. I stayed up, tossing and turning and worrying and speculating about the next day—what if Maura refused? Would Orlando stand up to her? Would I be left out on my own?—until eventually, as the morning hours drew in, I managed to nod off for a couple of hours.

I was woken up by a chilly breeze touching my face. I opened my eyes to a loft streaming with pale daylight. I heard the siblings' voices, faint. They weren't in the loft.

They were up on the roof. As I rubbed my eyes, coming to consciousness, I caught onto more of their conversation. They had already started discussing the issue. My stomach clenched. It didn't sound like it was going well so far.

Pushing aside my blanket, I crawled directly beneath the skylight and stood up, hoping to glean more of their conversation from this position. I didn't want them to think that I had woken up yet.

"We've worked so hard to get what we have," Maura was saying, her voice unsteady. "Why can't we just be happy with what we've built?"

"Happy?" Orlando spat back. "We're not happy, Maura. You've forgotten what happiness is."

"Happiness is peace," she replied pleadingly. "We have peace here. We've figured out how to get by. We have enough food to last us. We have a warm, dry shelter. We—"

"Like I said," Orlando steamrolled over her, "you've forgotten what happiness is."

There was a pause, as perhaps Maura was at a loss for words. I heard her blow out in exasperation. "Well, maybe I have, Orlando. Maybe I have!" At this point, it seemed that she had forgotten about me supposedly sleeping down here. Her voice rose to an almost desperate pitch. "But I'm not willing to risk what we have for something so… unreachable. You know what could happen if we got caught—"

"Yes, I know," Orlando growled. "But I would rather die fighting for something better than spend our final days in here, in 'peace'… rotting. We'll have enough time in our graves for that."

I was taken aback by the fire in his voice. When talking to him last night, he had appeared completely pessimistic, even right up until the end of our conversation. Maybe I had managed to spark something in him after all, more than I'd thought I had.

Maura didn't respond for a couple of minutes. I heard the sound of footsteps above me, pacing up and down.

"And all this… because of *her*?" Her tone was disbelieving now. "How can you even trust her? She's a total stranger. Even if we agreed to go along with her and help her find a phone, she could just be using us. She could abandon us the minute she manages to make contact with her family."

"She wouldn't do that," Orlando retorted so quickly and firmly, even I was taken aback.

"How can you say something like that?" Maura spluttered.

"I just... I just know, okay?" he shot back. "I can see through people. I know when someone's BSing me. I believe that she is from where she says she's from, and I believe that she will take us in, if we help her..." He drew in a deep breath. "Maura. Please. Let's at least *try* to live again."

Another pause. When Maura finally spoke again, this time, her voice was lower, deeper. "If I said no, would you leave with her, without me?" As she asked the question, she sounded like a child again, the way she had last night, when she had seemed afraid of being left alone. Clearly, the girl had abandonment issues.

Orlando groaned in irritation. "No, Maura! What makes you even ask that? Of course not. Of course I would not abandon you. That's why I'm busting my balls trying to convince you that we should do this. If we refuse, she might wander off by herself and then..."

His voice trailed off.

"And then *what*?" Maura asked.

"We'll never know what could have been," Orlando finished.

I waited with bated breath for Maura to respond.

"Okay," she said, eventually, in a voice so soft I barely heard it. "If this is what you want... then okay."

"I know we'd regret it if we didn't," Orlando said, sounding relieved.

"When would we leave?" Maura asked, tentative.

"I don't know. We need to talk to her."

As I heard them begin to make their way back to the skylight, I left the ladder and hurried back into bed. It would've been awkward if they'd thought I had just listened to the whole conversation. I quickly pulled the blanket over me and turned my back on them just before they climbed down the ladder and returned to the loft.

I sensed their gazes fall on me and slowly, I stretched out, allowing them to see me awake. Orlando was the first to catch my eye. Based on his expression, he seemed to already suspect that I had overheard everything.

Maura turned away and headed into the bathroom, leaving her brother and me alone.

"She agreed," he said, "in case you didn't hear." What I had sensed in Orlando's voice just now when he'd been talking to his sister up on the roof—life, a spark of passion—I now saw in his eyes as he continued: "If we're going to attempt this, then we should do it sooner rather than later. We ought to leave as soon as possible, right?"

"Right," I said. I nodded firmly, even as a chill ran down my spine.

Chapter 10: Grace

We began preparing to leave. Not knowing where everything was in their loft, I felt rather useless as I sat in one corner, watching while the two siblings went about pulling items from shelves and rummaging through their possessions. They gathered together three generously sized backpacks and started filling them up with food and water, followed by some clothes. They packed only one set of clothes for each of us, along with some waterproof overalls. I put on the warmest items from my outfit now, anticipating stepping outside. Next came the weapons: knives, guns and ammunition. These took up most of the backpacks' space.

"Oh, and matches," I said, "We need matches, or lighters—or both. Bring as many of those as you have."

Orlando grunted an agreement before heading to the chest of drawers and emptying it of about ten lighters and six boxes of matches. I only needed a single spark to brew up a fire, so what he had should be more than enough.

"Make sure you put the matches in a waterproof container," Maura said. She moved to the other side of the room and brought back three sturdy plastic boxes. "Put anything else that's water-sensitive in there too," she advised her brother. "Chances are we'll get soaked at some point."

Once the bags had been filled up, Orlando handed one to me. The siblings strapped their belts around their waists.

"We don't have a spare one of these," Orlando explained, gesturing to his belt, "so you'll just have to borrow mine. Like we did before."

I nodded, feeling queasy at the thought of having to zipline again.

"Now, we're almost done," Orlando muttered. "We need a map." He reached into a drawer and pulled out a map of Chicago. He planted it down on the table and spread it out. Maura and I peered over his shoulder. His finger traced from our current location to Lake Michigan. "The fence is supposed to run all the way along here," he said, continuing to glide his finger. "And there are posts, manned by IBSI members."

"Who are armed," Maura added, as if that would not have been obvious to me.

I sucked in a breath. *Okay...* Each of us stared at the map a few moments longer before Orlando folded it up and stuffed it into one of the waterproof boxes, where it would stay safe and dry. Then he picked up the blade-wheel and its remote.

"That's like... recharged and everything?" I asked, eyeing it nervously.

Orlando smirked darkly. "Yes."

I didn't know how that thing ran, whether on batteries or something else. "Where did you get that thing from?" I asked.

"I built it," Orlando replied.

"Seriously?"

He nodded, making his way with his sister toward the trap door. "Our father was an engineer, once upon a time.

I learned some stuff from him and managed to scrounge the components for it from a mixture of places—derelict stores and such…"

He bent down to lift open the trap door and extended the ladder to the ground. He climbed down first, followed by Maura and then me.

"Oh, wait," Maura said, as Orlando's feet touched the floor. "We're idiots."

"What?" I asked, anxious.

"Oh, yeah," Orlando said, apparently reading his sister's thoughts. "We forgot the helmets."

"Helmets?"

"Those gas mask things we were wearing," Orlando explained. "We have four of them, actually—we keep them in the largest cabinet, on top of the pile of clothes. Can you grab them?" he requested of me, since I was closest to the loft.

"Yeah." I climbed back up and found them quickly. "So what do we need these for, exactly?" I asked, climbing down the ladder and arriving next to the siblings.

"We use them like helmets," Orlando said. I handed one to each of them. They placed them over their heads, concealing their faces, while I pulled on mine. "They extend low enough to protect our necks… I'm sure I don't have to explain why that's useful."

Still keenly aware of the fang wounds in my leg, I nodded, gulping.

Chapter 11: Grace

We headed up the old stairwell toward the dreaded main roof of the building. I was already securing my heavy backpack around my shoulders, anticipating the glide. A spiteful wind whipped us as we strode out into the open. It was raining again—more heavily than when I had been outside with Orlando last night.

We did things in the same order as the day before. Maura was first to withdraw her hook, climb onto the ledge of the roof, and attach herself to the metal cable. She kicked off and swung gracefully, like the pro she was, to the neighboring skyscraper. Orlando followed her, threw me his belt once he reached the other side, and then it was my turn again.

I had done this enough times by now to know that it was better not to procrastinate. Before taking the leap this time, however, I focused my eyes on Orlando standing on the roof of the opposite building. I willed myself to remain fixed on him and not allow myself to glance down even for a moment as I launched myself off and went hurtling to the other side. I was still staring at Orlando's face with fierce determination when he reached down for me and helped me climb up onto the roof.

"Okay?" he asked, a touch of amusement in his eyes.

"Yeah."

We traveled across three streets in this manner before I spotted something in the sky, worryingly close. A helicopter. I could tell instantly from the build and shade of it that it was an IBSI helicopter. I had seen enough of them by now. It was the exact same type as the ones that had been sent to harass us in The Shade when we'd still had Lawrence in our midst.

"You see that, guys?" I asked the siblings nervously,

pointing to it. They glanced up, then shrugged and proceeded to glide to the next building. I had no choice but to follow them once Orlando had chucked his belt my way. I held my tongue, refraining from mentioning the helicopter again until it turned in the sky and began heading our way.

"Guys," I couldn't help but say again. "Are you sure that helicopter isn't something we should be worrying about?" I couldn't help but feel that the IBSI wouldn't just let me get away so easily after discovering that I had found out about the existence of FOEBA. But I did not want to let on to Maura and Orlando that I feared the hunters might be after me. It'd been difficult enough to get them to come with me on this mission in the first place. If they suspected that I was a prime target of the hunters, it would only increase their tensions—maybe not so much Orlando's, but definitely Maura's. I detected that even now she was coming only because her brother believed so strongly that they should. If it had been up to her, they wouldn't have budged from their loft.

"I think we all ought to be more concerned about what's on the ground than in the air," Maura said irritably. "Let's keep moving. We've got a lot more ground to cover."

With that, she swung herself to the next building. Before Orlando could follow her, I caught his arm and pulled him back. "Orlando," I said in a low voice. "I don't have a good feeling about this."

He turned on me. "What do you mean?"

"That's an IBSI helicopter. The IBSI is bad news all around. Both for me and for you."

"We've seen them around before and they haven't bothered us. What, exactly, are you worried about?" he asked, narrowing his eyes on me. He'd already clearly suspected that I was holding something back from him.

"Well, I did tell you before that I escaped from them. I'm not entirely sure that they would send an actual search party out for me... but they might."

Orlando swore beneath his breath. "This is the last thing we need."

"I know," I said, wincing. "But I think maybe we should try to stay a bit more inconspicuous. We're so easy to spot on these roofs."

"Maura isn't going to like this," he murmured before pushing himself off the ledge. By the time he'd thrown the belt back and I'd reached the other side, he had already broached the subject with his sister. Her expression was sour as she looked at me.

"You never mentioned that they might care about you enough to follow you," she said sharply. "You just said that you escaped from them."

"Well, I'm not necessarily saying that they do care that much. It's just a guess," I said, glancing once again up at the helicopter, which was drawing ever closer.

Quelling an argument before it could start, Orlando gripped his sister's arm and then my own. He pulled us both toward the peeling shelter covering the door that led down to the inside of the skyscraper we were perched on.

The door did not open easily, though thankfully, it wasn't locked. The three of us kicked against it and spilled inside, slamming the stiff door shut behind us.

"I really don't like this," Maura said, not making the slightest attempt to hide the discomfort in her tone. "This is not a good start to things."

"I agree that it's not," I said, gritting my teeth. "But I hope that I will be able to provide you both with a pretty good *end* to things."

Orlando made the blade-wheel fly beneath, and in front of, us as we descended the staircase, deeper into the building. We reached the bottom of the first flight of stairs, and found ourselves in a hallway. "I'm pretty sure there are Bloodless in this building," Orlando said. "So keep a sharp eye and ear."

I reached into my backpack and pulled out a lighter, my thumb resting on the flint wheel, at the ready.

We traveled further along the corridor and then took to another staircase.

"So if we're not going to take the quickest route over the roofs, which route will we take?" Maura asked her brother. At least she sounded resigned and less resentful this time.

"We'll have to wind our way through the streets for a bit," her brother replied, his eyes fixed firmly in front of us. "At least until the chopper has gone away."

Somehow, I doubted there would only be one.

Let's just hope that they do go away, I prayed in my mind. *They need to think that I died in that river.*

I also had to hope that we really would be safer on the ground than up there. That there wouldn't be swarms of hunters searching the streets. Because we'd be faced with enough obstacles down below—namely the Bloodless and the bloodthirsty gangs of convicts—without having to fear every corner we turned that we would bump into a crowd of IBSI members.

As my mind began to spiral into thinking about all the awful things that might happen on ground level, I very quickly realized that if I wanted to stand any chance of escaping this place with my sanity intact, I could not think of anything but the present. I had to become like an animal—go on my raw instincts at every turn, and be alert at all times.

"I knew it," Orlando said suddenly, raising a hand. My eyes shot toward where he was pointing. We had just emerged on the twelfth floor of the building—according to a helpful sign. At the end of the hallway we were standing on was a lanky pale body crouched over another lanky, pale body. Two Bloodless on top of each other.

At first I thought… well, probably what most people would think if they saw two naked bodies pressed against one another. But I soon realized that was *definitely* not the case. The Bloodless on top looked like it was eating the other. Biting into its neck, creating a sickening squelching sound. It appeared to be so consumed with what it was doing that it had not even noticed us yet. Orlando grabbed my hand and Maura's and quickly pulled us back into the stairwell, where we rushed to continue our journey down the building.

It must have sensed us—I knew how sharp Bloodless' senses were—but simply found us less interesting in that moment. How could that be? It was a shocking sight to behold. I'd never thought that Bloodless preyed on their own kind.

My throat was hoarse as I asked, "Why was it doing that?"

Maura and Orlando, although their breathing had quickened as we hurried down the stairs, hardly seemed surprised by it at all.

"Most likely the one on the bottom had recently preyed on someone," Orlando replied in between pants. "The one on top detected blood in it and managed to bring it down. As I said, this city is a place of desperation. Sometimes Bloodless who are particularly vicious and starved will attack their own kind and rip at them, attempting to suck out any blood they might have consumed in a recent meal."

My God.

Screeching echoed down the stairwell.

Maura groaned. "Great. It's had second thoughts."

My instinct was to immediately increase my speed, but the first thing that Maura and Orlando did was stop completely. "There is no point whatsoever in running now," Orlando said, a steely expression in his gaze as he looked up the stairs.

And he was right. We didn't stand a chance in hell of getting far with this creature. It was leaping ten steps at a time and reached us within a matter of seconds—just in time for me to fumble with my lighter and spark up a flame.

I sent a blast shooting in the monster's direction. It screeched again and staggered back, at which point Orlando set the blade-wheel hurtling toward it at full speed. As the sharp knives made contact with the Bloodless' body, it practically exploded from the force, splattering us and everything around us with blood and mushy pieces of limb.

My stomach clenched as Orlando's blade-wheel completed its task. The Bloodless' body had been mangled as though it had been put through a grinder and spread all over the staircase.

I sure hope I don't piss off Orlando one of these days...

Taking in the nauseating sight, I gained a whole new appreciation for the clunky gas mask that I was wearing.

"If there are two in this building, there will be more," Maura said.

Her words proved to be true within less than a minute. Whatever Bloodless were present in this building appeared to have been summoned by the commotion—and we heard the sound of clattering on the levels both above and beneath us. Then terrifyingly fast footsteps on the metal stairs. Two crowds of the murderous creatures came into view, both above and beneath us on the staircase.

No! I couldn't believe this was happening. I had expected us to get a little bit further into our journey before having to deal with this level of crap. We had only just left the loft and already we were surrounded by dozens of Bloodless. I feared that the siblings' blade might not be able to handle them all.

Maura, who had pulled out two guns from her backpack, began firing at both groups. She appeared to be aiming primarily at the Bloodless' skulls, but also smattering bullets into their chests and necks. I already knew that bullets weren't an effective way to deal with Bloodless—they had to be completely dismembered or burnt to ashes in order to end them. Her bullets were clearly a painful annoyance to them, however, and it helped distract them. But the real work had to be done by me and Orlando.

Orlando revved the rotor blades and sent them soaring to the Bloodless above us. I pressed down hard on my lighter's flint wheel, coaxing the fire into my palm. I made it blaze up into a deadly billow and scorched the staircase, surprising some Bloodless so much they jolted back. Others willingly dove down the stairwell to escape my heat. But the more tenacious among them kept trying to get at us, even despite the flames. They backed up a bit before relaunching an attack, hoping to catch me off guard.

I couldn't tell how many I managed to burn, since it was hard to see by now. It was dark as it was, and the smoke was beginning to impair my vision. But soon, the screeching lessened on my side, giving me confidence to relinquish my flames just a little and turn to my right to check on how Maura and Orlando were doing. There appeared to be a lot more attacking from their side, since they were still tackling the crowd.

"Orlando," I yelled, "watch out!" One of the Bloodless had taken to the ceiling to dodge the blades. He was crawling above Orlando and looked like he was on the verge of pouncing.

Orlando's reflexes were slower than mine on this occasion. I launched myself at him, shoving him out of the way, before engulfing the offending Bloodless with my flames.

Catching fire, it dropped from the ceiling and rolled down the stairs, attempting to put itself out.

More Bloodless attempted to pull off the same ceiling trick, but Orlando was more alert now. And so was I. I kept my fire directed at the ceiling while Orlando made the blade hover up and down in a constant whizzing motion to slash the Bloodless both ducking and leaping on the stairs... until Bloodless stopped approaching. We had fought them off... for now.

By now, we found ourselves standing in puddles of Bloodless stew. And the walls were completely coated with their juices.

Orlando caught my eye. His chest was heaving, his

breathing coming in dry pants.

"Thanks," he croaked.

I nodded, stoic. "I owed you one."

Chapter 12: Grace

"Are we still honestly going to keep heading down to the ground?" Maura queried disbelievingly. "We're only, like, halfway down the building and look what we've just met with."

Orlando heaved a sigh. And I felt guilty. It was only because of me that we were forced to head downstairs. The IBSI weren't a big threat to the siblings, or so they believed.

"Well," I said, wetting my lower lip. "Maybe we could just wait here a while until the chopper's gone out of sight."

Orlando exhaled in impatience. He shifted on his feet, looking left and right along the corridor we had emerged in after leaving the Bloodless-soaked stairwell.

"All right. We'll hang around for a bit."

We moved back up the building cautiously, hoping we wouldn't come across more Bloodless. We needed to climb fairly high up so that we could get a good view of the sky without actually being on the roof. We found a small janitor's room on the top floor that had a skylight. Orlando pushed a desk that lined one of the walls until it was directly beneath the glass. Being the tallest, he climbed on top of it and gazed out.

Maura and I waited tensely as he looked around.

"Nope," he said. "There's still one hovering near this area… Oh, wait, and there's another one, too."

Crap. I balled my sweating hands. Were they really going to go away anytime soon? *I have to get out of this city.* How long would it be before they started sweeping the buildings looking for me? Would they really go that far? Suddenly, staying put didn't seem like a good idea at all.

"Okay, maybe we should just keep moving," Orlando said. He returned to the floor and looked from me to his sister, who was scowling. "We got an unlucky start," he said. "But I don't think waiting is going to make any difference. For all we know, things could just get worse."

Maura pursed her lips, making no attempt to hide her disdain, but said nothing.

So we left the janitor's room. Thankfully, we didn't come across any more Bloodless on our way down to the ground floor. I hoped we'd had our share of them for at least the next hour. My nerves were still quivering from the monsters.

We moved to the entrance of the building and stepped out into the wet street. Thankfully it appeared to be empty.

"So now which way?" I asked in a whisper.

"The river," Orlando replied beneath his breath. "Traveling along the river is the best way to remain safe from Bloodless because they can't stand whatever it's been contaminated with."

The river. "That runs so close to IBSI's headquarters though," I murmured.

"Part of it does," Orlando said, "but that part isn't where we keep our raft. So we won't need to pass their base."

Orlando took a right turn. Maura and I quickly

followed behind him as he began heading down the street. All three of us gazed around, alert like animals for the presence of our numerous predators.

The slicing of helicopter blades in the sky was disconcertingly loud. The hunters were still close. We tried to keep out of view as much as we could, sticking close to the buildings and moving beneath ledges.

"How much longer until the river?" I couldn't help but ask. It felt like we had been traveling for about an hour, though I doubted it had been more than ten minutes.

"We're not far. Another five minutes or so," Orlando replied.

"Oh, no," Maura hissed, pointing up the street. "Bloodless."

Indeed there were. I spotted a whole crowd of them, huddled in a circle and apparently piling on top of something. A meal, I assumed.

"We'll have to take a detour now," Orlando said, frustrated.

We tried to back away unnoticed, but that was a futile attempt. Some of the creatures had already noticed us. They tore away from whatever they were ravaging up the road and began loping toward us. I didn't need to use my flames this time, though. Orlando was prepared enough. He sent the blade-wheel hurtling toward them, and it spliced them before they could reach within twelve feet of us.

We hurried onward before more Bloodless could decide to have a go at us. We slipped down a narrow, winding alleyway and reappeared on the other side, onto another wide street. This one clearly had once been posh. It was lined with expensive designer shops and restaurants with prestigious names. There was also an old hotel whose windows were smashed in, its rotating doorway mangled.

We raced to the end of this road and onto the road parallel to it. Here, to my relief, I spotted water. A dark, murky river. A barrier had been erected, lining the river's edge. The three of us climbed over it and touched down in squelching mud.

Orlando pointed toward a wide, steel bridge, a little further up. "We left our raft just beneath that," he explained.

We fought our way through the muddy, narrow bank until we reached the shelter of the bridge. As I eyed the contraption that was leaning against the bridge's wall, I could very well see why Orlando had said that it would be generous to call it a boat. It was simply a raft, constructed from logs of wood and tied together with rope. It looked shaky and precarious. I felt nervous at the idea of riding on that, especially since the river was rough in this torrential weather. But at least this time, even if I fell in, my hands would not be tied and I would be able to swim.

The siblings tugged on the raft, placing it over the water, before the three of us climbed onto it. Orlando reached for a tall stick that had lain beside the raft on the bank. Dipping half of it into the water, he pushed us away from the edge and toward the center of the river. The current soon picked us up and began washing us away.

"So," I said tensely, my voice echoing as we passed beneath the bridge, "is the IBSI's base behind us?"

"Yes," Maura replied. "Close behind us."

"This river would lead us to Lake Michigan," Orlando informed me, "if a barrier had not been erected. As I said, it's impossible to pass through it by waterway, so once we get nearer, we're going to have to head back to the bank and travel the rest of the way on foot... somehow. But this is the safest place to be for now. We're away from the Bloodless, and it will be harder for gangs to give us trouble. Assuming we don't bump into them on the river itself."

After reaching the other end of the bridge and gliding out into the open, I really wished that bridge had been wider. This river, although less so than the roofs of the buildings, was still uncomfortably exposed to the sky. We were moving along swiftly but still, it would not be very difficult for hunters to spot us.

It seemed that Orlando was sharing my thoughts as we both glanced up at a chopper circling a cluster of skyscrapers in the distance. For now, it was apparently preoccupied and there weren't any other aircrafts around that we could spot. We had to hope that we could slip by inconspicuously, and the hunters in the chopper would remain distracted by whatever it was they were doing—or watching—over there.

***

I was actually surprised by the steadiness of the raft, how it supported all of our weight. But that was the best thing I could say about it. It was wet—horribly wet. The river water washed over the logs, drenching my feet and making me feel even colder. At least we'd packed waterproof overalls, which saved us from getting completely soaked to the bone by the rain pounding down over our heads.

The journey was also slower than I would've liked it to be. We got stuck occasionally, and other times the current was too strong and we had to pause by the edge for a while before continuing.

I could not say how many miles we had traveled, but we'd made a fair bit of headway down the river by the time a second helicopter came into view—flying closer to us than the other we'd spotted. It was hovering over the buildings, several miles away, but it looked like we were in danger of it turning toward us.

"I think it's time to get back to the bank," I said, eyeing it.

Neither of the siblings were happy about the idea, but Orlando, using the long stick, navigated us to the river's edge. I clambered onto the bank with Maura and then the two of us helped Orlando drag the raft out of the water.

Trees lined this part of the river. We found a trunk to lean the raft against before making our way to a bus shelter on the road. We sat down beneath the covering on a plastic bench. Orlando reached into his backpack and pulled out the map which he'd kept in one of the waterproof containers. He spread it out. "Hm." He studied it for a couple of minutes before folding it up again and replacing it. "Right. I think I know the best route to take, though I hate these parts. The closer we are to the shore, the more likely we are to run into trouble."

We left the bus stop. Thunder broke out overhead, and I caught a flash of lightning. It had been raining nonstop ever since we'd left Maura and Orlando's loft, but this was the heaviest rainfall we'd experienced so far. A severe wind lashed us.

"Augh," Maura moaned. "I hate this weather."

In spite of all three of us beginning to shiver, we plowed on for several miles. We came across more Bloodless in the streets but thankfully, Orlando's blade wheel was still holding up well, and he could deal with them on his own. After three hours, Orlando suggested that we stop for a short break.

"I'm starving," Maura agreed.

I was also feeling exhausted. This damp weather, even though I was covered in plastic and wore a mask over my head, had a way of penetrating to your bones.

Orlando seemed to already have a clear idea where we ought to stop. He wasn't gazing around at the buildings wondering; his eyes were trained ahead. He led us directly to the end of the road and then stopped outside an old church—a church that was still beautiful even despite its disrepair. Although many of its stained-glass windows had been smashed, its thick stone walls were intact, and to my surprise, so was the heavy wooden door.

"We'll go in here," Orlando said.

He gripped the door handle and pushed it open. We stepped in cautiously and found ourselves looking around a derelict, yet hauntingly beautiful chapel. Pale orange light trickled through the tinted panes that remained intact surrounding the engraved, concave ceiling. Swaths of deep green ivy spilled in through the lower, glassless windows, and trailed down the walls to touch the dusty, stone floors. Faded rosewood benches lined the church, some upturned, others almost too perfectly in place. Pigeons fluttered in the church's heights, soaring from one broad balcony to the other. Their flapping and soft cooing were the only sounds to stir the eerie silence.

The air in here was chill, but at least it was mostly dry. Orlando closed the door behind us as we removed our masks. We moved slowly to one of the benches and sat down. Maura dug a hand into her backpack and withdrew a can of lentils. She cracked it open and began pouring the contents into her mouth directly—as though she were drinking a soda—since none of us had brought spoons.

I pitied Orlando as he pulled out a can from his own bag. Being in charge of the blade wheel, he was constantly carrying around a heavy remote. Plus, he'd been the one with the strenuous task of navigating us down the river. He must have been starved, too.

I supposed that I also ought to eat something. Although my stomach was aching, it was hard to tell whether that was from hunger or just from the sheer angst I had been in for the past… I had lost track of how many hours by now. Probably a mixture of both. I opened one of my cans and began to munch.

Orlando was the first to finish. He placed his empty can in a plastic bag and replaced it in his backpack. Then he stood, his eyes traveling around the church. He began to wander along the aisle, toward the other end of the chapel. I glanced furtively at Maura as he left us. She was watching him.

It felt like Maura and I had gotten off to an unnecessarily bad start and I didn't like the undertones of tension that existed between us. But I didn't know what I could do—if there was even anything that I could do—to solve that. Now wasn't the time to be worrying about that though.

I refocused on my lentils. I had only eaten half, but I was not hungry anymore. Still, wasting food would be a mortal sin in this city, so I forced myself to finish them.

Maura had finished her food by now. She leaned back on her bench, her legs stretched out, her eyes half closed, relaxing.

I looked around for Orlando. He now had reached the end of the church and, to my surprise, was kneeling before the altar. Orlando hadn't exactly struck me as the religious type.

I stood up and made my way to him, my footsteps echoing off the stone. Orlando had one hand over his heart as he knelt. I didn't want to disturb him. I took a seat on the bench behind him and admired the painted apse.

After five minutes or so, Orlando stirred. He rose to his feet and turned. His expression was stony, his eyes a tad glazed. He sat down next to me on the bench.

"Are you a Christian?" I asked.

He shook his head. "Can't consider myself one," he replied hoarsely. He cast a glance back at Maura, who was still resting. He joined me in gazing at the altar. "I've never been a person of faith… At least, not until I murdered a man." His fingers locked, and he cracked his knuckles. "It's not something you can easily forget," he went on, "You know? Not something you can just will to the back of your mind. No matter how much you try to tell yourself that it was self-defense, or that it was justified somehow… the guilt doesn't go away."

I nodded, unsure of what to say, or whether he expected me to say anything at all. Somehow, I doubted it.

"Hey, you guys going to come back here?" Maura called, apparently rousing from her half-slumber and interrupting her brother's and my awkward pause.

"Yes," Orlando muttered, barely loud enough for her to hear.

The two of us returned to her. She was already replacing her backpack over her shoulders. "We should probably keep moving," she said.

"Yeah," Orlando agreed again thickly, before donning his own backpack.

The sudden slamming of a door made us all jump. Our first instinct was to look behind us—to the main entrance—but there was nobody there.

"Who are you?" A man's voice echoed through the

chapel. It came from behind us, but above us. Our eyes shot to one of the balconies. A couple was gazing down at us, a man and a woman. They had short-cropped hair, the two of them, and they were pale, just like Maura and Orlando.

Orlando grabbed Maura's and my hands and backed away with us toward the exit. I caught a glimpse of Maura's hand sliding over the gun in her belt.

"Who are *you*?" Orlando shot back.

The man grabbed the woman and disappeared. Orlando and Maura exchanged glances. We were about to leave when footsteps sounded on a staircase and the couple emerged on our level. They walked toward us cautiously. I realized now how terribly thin they were—even thinner than Maura and Orlando. They had black shadows beneath their eyes, and looked on the verge of starvation.

"I didn't mean to scare you," he said, eyeing Maura's gun and Orlando's wheel of death. "This church is our shelter."

"And it has been ours for the past half hour," Orlando replied. "But we're leaving now."

"Do you know why we're here?" the man asked, desperation in his tone.

"No," Orlando replied, drawing us closer to the door. "I don't know why we're here." He gripped the handle and pulled.

"Wait!" the woman pleaded, rushing forward and pushing the door shut. She clutched Orlando's arm. "Please, help us. We just woke up a couple of days ago. Found ourselves in this hellhole! Our heads shaven. No food. Nothing to defend ourselves with. Please!"

He withdrew from her, shaking her aside. "It's every man for himself around here," he said coldly. "You're going to have to make your own way. Find your own food, your own weapons, just like my sister and I did. Consider yourself lucky you have each other."

"We can't go out there!" the man exclaimed.

"We've tried already," the woman gasped. She looked on the verge of tears.

I couldn't help but feel moved by the state of these two people, even though they were total strangers. I thought about the canned food that I had in my backpack. Did I really need all that? I had felt full after just half a can of lentils. I'd had to force myself to finish the rest. I was sure that I could spare at least one tin. That would be better than nothing for them...

I slipped my backpack off my shoulders and planted it on the floor. But as I unzipped my food compartment and dipped a hand inside, Maura and Orlando turned on me.

"What the hell are you doing?" Maura hissed.

Orlando stooped down to me and gripped my arm, stalling it in place. His deep, dark eyes dug into mine as he uttered a single word. "Don't."

I did realize that this wasn't exactly my food to give. So it was a bit presumptuous of me to offer some to these people without asking for permission. I glanced apologetically toward the couple… in time to see the man stoop for a broken bench leg and bring it hurtling forward to strike Orlando in the back.

"Orlando!" I screamed, instinctively lurching for him. I careened into him in time to send him flying out of the way. The two of us went crashing to the ground, myself on top of him.

A gunshot sounded.

"No, Maura!" Orlando bellowed, deafeningly loud in my ear. He shoved me off of him and leapt to his feet. But by the time he did, it was too late. Maura had already shot a bullet into the shoulder of the man, and as she tightened her grip on the gun, she was clearly about to end him.

Orlando threw himself at her and gripped her wrist, forcing the gun from her hands before she could fire the final shot.

She struggled to grab the gun back. "He would have killed you if he'd gotten the chance!" Maura yelled. "All of us, for our supplies!"

Orlando, breathing heavily, turned to face the man who was lying on the ground. He was groaning in agony, clutching one shoulder, with his partner bending over him and sobbing.

Orlando's eyes returned to Maura and he replied through gritted teeth, "Not. In. Here."

She looked like she was going to continue arguing, but he didn't give her the chance. He stooped to pick up his wheel and backpack again, and handed me my bag. I glanced worriedly at the injured man. Their chances of survival had looked practically nil to begin with... now, with him injured, I wondered if they'd survive the next few hours.

But it seemed that this was life in Bloodless Chicago.

Every man for himself.

"Let's go," Orlando grunted, herding his sister and me through the door. "We've dishonored this place enough."

Chapter 13: Grace

"Take that as a lesson not to feed people around here," Maura said to me as we marched on through the rain, away from the church.

"When people get this desperate, they're like wild animals," Orlando explained in a low tone.

Still feeling shaken by the ordeal, I tried to turn my thoughts to other matters. *Lake Michigan. A phone.* I'd had enough of all of this. I just wanted out of this nightmare. Oh, how I wished that it really was all a bad dream. My chest ached as I thought of home. The Shade. My beautiful, safe island. My family. My friends. I felt like an idiot for ever leaving… and yet I hadn't been able to fight the urge. Once I had gotten a whiff of Lawrence and Georgina's mystery, I'd just had to follow the trail.

They don't say curiosity killed the cat for no reason, I thought to myself, grinding my teeth. *What a stupid, stupid cat I am.*

All of us fell silent for the next hour as we continued through the city. We passed a few more small groups of Bloodless—about three or four at a time—which weren't too strenuous to get rid of, thanks to Orlando's trusty wheel. I could still hear helicopters overhead, but this part of the city had more trees, and I was less concerned about being spotted from the air. Orlando kept stopping every now and then to consult the map to verify we weren't traveling off course.

When he estimated we had about thirty minutes left before approaching the IBSI's fences that bordered the shore, we all stopped short. My worst fears came to pass at the end of a long boulevard.

Tanks. IBSI tanks.

They were positioned at the cross section of our road and the next. And there were hunters out of the vehicles—covered in armor and carrying heavy weapons. My heart was in my throat as we leapt behind a tree to hide. I prayed that none of them had spotted us… or detected us.

Oh, no. Orlando had warned me already of the dangers.

So far we'd had to deal with our fair share of Bloodless, but had been lucky enough to not be targeted by any gangs. But now… these guys. I would take the gangs any day over these men.

"What do you think they are doing?" Maura breathed so quietly, I could barely hear her.

Orlando shrugged. "This area by the shore is always more populated with IBSI members. Should hardly be a surprise to come across them now."

We peered out cautiously through the leaves of the low-hanging branches. We could see more from this angle, low to the ground, than when we had been standing on the sidewalk. I spotted about ten hunters gathered in the middle of the road—they were easy to recognize, because they all wore the same thing… but now I spotted one other man, too, who wasn't dressed in uniform. He was dressed in worn, mismatched clothing, the type that Maura and Orlando sported.

"Oh." Orlando let out a breath. "Th-That's Paul. Paul Stokes."

"Who's Paul Stokes?" I asked in a strained whisper.

"Are you sure?" Maura asked Orlando fearfully, bulldozing over my question.

"Yes," Orlando hissed. "Can't you see?"

Maura's eyes narrowed, then her jaw dropped. "Oh, my God. Yes. That's him."

"Who is Paul Stokes?" I urged.

"He's a gang leader," Orlando whispered. "One of the worst."

"*The* worst," Maura breathed. "His gang is the largest and most brutal of all of them."

"What's he doing talking to the IBSI?" I wondered.

"Your guess is as good as ours," Orlando replied.

"Whatever they're doing," Maura said, "we need to take a different route. I don't feel like sitting around here much longer. Ugh." She gestured to our backsides, now covered in muck and rainwater from dropping down on the damp soil that lined the sidewalk.

Orlando pointed to our right, to a crack between two buildings—an alleyway, only wide enough for one person to enter at a time. Orlando, positioning his wheel sideways, went first. Then Maura and I darted after him.

"How are we ever going to get around them?" Maura

whispered. "We don't have a clue what we're doing, do we? We don't know how to even reach the fence, let alone the shore."

Orlando didn't respond and neither did I, though I was sure that we were both sharing Maura's thoughts. Reaching the end of the alleyway, Orlando looked left and right and then nodded to us, indicating that it was safe to step out.

"I think what we need to do now is figure out where the IBSI's posts are along the fence," Orlando said. "Obviously, those are going to be the hardest to penetrate." He gazed around at the buildings on this road. "We need to climb to the top of one of these buildings and get high up again. I reckon from there we'll be able to make out the fence. I'm sure we're close enough—"

Orlando stopped short, his eyes falling on his sister. She had moved a few feet away from us, toward a lamp post, and was staring at it, open-mouthed. She was looking at a sign. A sign that made my skin erupt in goosebumps.

I staggered closer to it with Orlando, gaping. Barely believing my eyes. Praying and wishing that somehow this wasn't real. But it was.

I was standing face-to-face with a photograph of myself,

or rather, a screen capture. I was in a familiar place—in one of the hallways of the IBSI's Chicago base—and I was frozen in a running stance, my right foot forward, my hands chained in front of me. My sweaty, panic-stricken face had been zoomed in on, my every feature clearly visible.

Above the photograph read the bold red words:

"*WANTED.*

Contact your nearest IBSI scout with any information.
REWARD: Treatment and release."

All the blood drained from my face. I forgot how to breathe.

The three of us stood in stunned silence.

Then Maura backed away from the sign. Turning on me, she looked me over with an expression that chilled me to the core.

Her eyes shot to her brother.

"Treatment and release," she said breathlessly. "*Treatment* and release!"

As suddenly as everything had just occurred, somehow, I was already prepared for what was about to happen. It was every man for himself out here, after all, wasn't it? Orlando had said it himself.

Maura cast another fleeting glance at me, and the next thing I knew, she had bolted into the narrow alleyway... back in the direction of the hunters.

Chapter 14: Grace

As much as every instinct I had within me urged me to go racing after Maura, attempt to somehow stop her, my feet remained rooted to the spot. My mind was frozen in shock. In fear. In panic.

Orlando was a blur as he zoomed after her without even a backward glance at me.

They're going to turn me in.

They would be fools not to.

They will get treatment and release!

What person wouldn't leap at this?

Move, Grace! You have to move! In a few minutes from

now, this road is going to be teeming with hunters. I had to make it on my own from now on. I had to find somewhere to hide.

As I raced away from the alleyway entrance and loped across the road toward the opposite sidewalk, I tried to bring some sanity to my frenzied thoughts and focus on the things that I still had to my advantage.

I still have my backpack. I still have lighters and matches. I have fire. Somehow, I just needed to wait around this area and stay undetected, and find a way to slip through to the other side of the fence. At least I had been able to travel this far with Maura and Orlando through the city. I should be grateful I hadn't had to do that all alone. I wasn't far from the shore now. *There has to be a way to get out! There has to—*

My desperate ramblings were interrupted by a hiss behind me, coming from the other side of the road.

"Grace!"

I dared shoot a glance back to see that it was Orlando. He had returned to the sidewalk, and he was standing with a struggling Maura in his grip.

He furrowed his heavy brows at me, mirroring my own confusion.

"Where are you going?" he mouthed.

Where am I going?

Where AM I going?

Shock and confusion rolled over me before a swell of relief rose in my chest. Orlando hadn't left to join his sister in ratting me out. He had gone to bring her back!

But why?

What kind of crazy person was he?

Even as he continued to fight with his sister, he beckoned me over to them. I approached cautiously, watching as he clamped a hand over Maura's mouth as she tried to call out.

"Maura!" he seethed. "Don't. Do. This."

Fury flashed in Maura's eyes as she glared at her brother. "Have you lost your damn mind?" she managed beneath Orlando's hand. "Get off me!"

Orlando kept her mouth smothered. His eyes dug into hers just as severely. "Do you honestly believe those people?" he whispered. "Do you honestly believe that they'll give you treatment—the same people who put us in this hellhole to begin with?"

"What is the risk?" she panted. "There is none! Even if they're lying, it can only help us to get in their good graces."

"You're an idiot, Maura!" Orlando snarled. "Good graces? You think these people even have good graces? Look at what they're doing to people here!"

"But—"

"And even if they gave us treatment," Orlando bulldozed on, "and cured us of whatever the hell they have infected us with in the first place… they would release us where? Into what?"

At this, Maura faltered. She stopped struggling so much. Orlando removed his hand from her mouth slowly. "You don't think things through, do you?" he went on. "They would release us back out into the world where we are convicted criminals—sentenced to death."

"But… they could waive that punishment for us," Maura croaked. Although she had started arguing her case again, at least now she was being quieter about it. "They obviously have a lot of sway with the government. They could grant us immunity from our crimes."

My stomach tensed as Orlando paused. Terror gripped me as I thought that perhaps his sister had managed to turn him over to her line of thinking. His expression became stony, unreadable. He gulped. But then he shook his head.

"They didn't state that on the sign—I'm sure they would have, considering all of us here have come from Death Row. But even if they offered immunity, making a deal with them like this… It just doesn't feel right."

"What? Doesn't feel right?" Maura wheezed, and I realized that she had tears in her eyes now. She was so desperate she was begging her brother. When he didn't respond, she shook him. "Nothing feels right about our situation, dammit! This is the only thing that could make us right!"

Orlando exhaled sharply, clutching her hands and shoving them down from his chest. "The outside world would never welcome back murderers," he replied.

"Uncle would take us in," Maura pleaded.

"But would he? We don't even know if he's still alive. He was in a hospital with stage-four liver cancer, Maura. We don't even know how much time has passed since we got taken from jail. We can't rely on his open arms. And without him, we would never find a home outside—and who would employ us? How would we survive? What would be there to stop us from sinking back into our old habits? Would you be able to resist?" He glared daggers at her.

Her lips quivered, moving to say, "Yes," but not quite managing it.

Orlando's burning eyes flickered to me momentarily, before returning to his sister. "Grace has offered us a place in The Shade. A place where we don't have to worry about food, shelter, or safety. We might not get the IBSI's treatment, but I for one would rather spend the last days, or months, or years—neither you nor I can say how much longer we have—in a place of beauty and peace, than pass a longer life in hell."

Maura scoffed scornfully. "Oh, The Shade. It sounds like heaven. A land of rainbows and roses. I, too, would rather spend the last of my life there than go back to our old life. And yes, maybe Grace would allow us to reside on the island, but—" Here, she broke down, tears spilling from her eyes—tears of desperation, tears of sheer exhaustion. She sank to her knees. "Let's face it, Orlando. We're never going to get past the fence. We're never going to make it to the shore!"

Deep voices sounded on the other side of the alleyway.

Orlando stooped to his sister and scooped her up before meeting my eyes. He nodded toward a derelict hotel on the opposite side of the road. I picked up his blade wheel and carried it for him while we dashed across the street and hurried inside the hotel.

Orlando and I were silent, Maura still sobbing quietly against her brother's shoulder, as we hurried up a dusty staircase. We wound our way upward—thankfully meeting no Bloodless on the stairs—until we could climb no further. We found ourselves emerging in a long hallway lined with doors that led to what I guessed would be luxury suites.

Orlando barged into one toward the end of the corridor, one whose lock had been broken. Indeed, this was a suite, a two-bedroom suite by the looks of it. I closed the door behind us, and we moved to the furthest room in the apartment, locking ourselves inside. Orlando laid his sister down on the bed. Her sobbing subsided, and her wet, pale face took on a glazed, dead expression. She curled up into a fetal position, then shut her eyes tight, as though the world around her was just too much to cope with right now.

Orlando sank down on the edge of the double bed, heaving a sigh and dropping his face into his hands.

I wasn't sure what to do with myself. Although half of me was still swimming in relief that the siblings had not turned me over to the IBSI, the other half of me felt guilty. Painfully so. These people were placing all their hopes on me. Me, when I didn't have the foggiest clue what I was doing or how I was going to lead them to my so-called promised land.

And now I really was in deep crap. Not only did I know for certain that the IBSI was fully committed to hunting me down, but they were also recruiting a selection of the worst, most dangerous criminals in the whole United States to help them do it.

Great. They really, really care about this FOEBA thing...

Still, more than ever, fire burned within me—I had not just myself to think about. I held these two fragile lives in the palms of my hands—people I owed my own life to several times over.

I planted the blade-wheel down on the floor and moved to the dirt-smeared window. I brushed against the glass with my sleeve, attempting to clear it. Gazing through, I was met with the most welcome sight I had beheld since arriving in this black, hopeless city.

Water. Lake Michigan. It took my breath away to realize just how close we were to it—only a few streets away. But as my eyes roamed the streets... they were teeming with men and women. They appeared to be predominantly IBSI members, but I also spotted some others who, judging by their attire, were obviously inmates of Bloodless Chicago like Maura and Orlando. And there was a fence. A high, electric fence with nasty barbs lining its top. It stretched for as far as I could see along the shore.

We were so close... yet so, so far.

Now more than ever in my life, how I wished that I had inherited my father's powers of flight. The ability to thin myself, soar wherever I wished. If only I had more of his genes in me, I never would have found myself in this place to start with. I would...

A thought struck me like a bludgeon, stalling my pointless regrets.

I spun around and looked at Orlando's blade wheel. That thing could fly. It was sturdy, too. Sturdy enough to slice through packs of Bloodless and leave them in nothing but mangled pieces.

My breath hitched as I fought to keep my hopes down. If I let them rise, the disappointment would crush me to dust.

"Orlando," I croaked, moving to the wheel and picking it up. It had a grip in the center of it, in between all of the outward-pointing blades, which allowed a person to hold it safely. The grip was also wide enough for two hands to clamp comfortably over it.

Orlando's eyes rose to me, his eyelids heavy. "What?" he asked.

"Th-This wheel can fly," I began to stammer. "Could it—"

Orlando had already guessed where I was going with this. To my dismay, he shook his head immediately. "That thing couldn't carry you."

"Are you sure?" I asked.

"I know what I built, Grace," he said, irritated now. "And I don't suggest that you try it. It would be dangerous. It's not made to take that kind of pressure. One of the blades could come loose and go driving into you."

I hesitated. "Really?"

"Really."

"It's just that," I dared to go on, "they look pretty secure in their places to me."

"So you're saying you want to try it?" he asked, raising his brows.

Is that what I'm saying? I glanced at the razor-sharp knives and gulped. "Yes," I replied. *Can one achieve anything in life without risk?*

Orlando stared at me, then raised his hands in the air. "Okay. Okay. Try it if you really dare. Just don't blame me if you get a limb sliced off."

Yeah…

I moved to the center of the room with the blade, a safe distance away from the siblings, and raised it above my head. Orlando picked up the remote, still eyeing me doubtfully as if half hoping I would have second thoughts at the last minute. I pursed my lips, indicating that I was about to do no such thing, even though inside of me I was wincing.

"You ready?" he murmured.

"Yup," I said, clipped. *As ready as I'll ever be to have a dozen freaking samurai blades spinning less than a foot from my skull.*

"Okay…" Orlando moved a dial, and the rotor began to spin. The blades picked up speed, flying terrifyingly close to my ears. They sent air beating down my neck. My pulse raced at twice its speed. My hands began to sweat so much I feared I'd lose grip and then… I felt a sudden lift. A tiny one—enough to raise me a fraction of a centimeter above the ground before my soles flattened again—but a lift nonetheless.

Orlando switched off the wheel. The blades slowed.

"Wait!" I said. "Didn't you see that? It lifted me a bit! Try again!"

Orlando rolled his eyes. "I put it at full speed already. Whatever small lift you felt is the maximum it's capable of. I told you. It's not strong enough."

"But… Maybe I'm just too heavy."

"Uh, yeah," Orlando said, his tone dripping with sarcasm. "That's one explanation."

"I mean, maybe it could lift someone lighter." My eyes immediately moved to Maura. I felt guilty and out of place to dare suggest that she try such a dangerous stunt but… I couldn't help myself. "What if Maura tried it? She's a lot shorter than me, and she's way slimmer, too."

Maura stirred at her name. She sat up on the bed and looked at me. Her eyes were still glazed, distant, as though a part of her was still locked away in her shell.

To my surprise, she murmured, "I'll try it."

Orlando cast me an annoyed look. "You know it's dangerous, Maura. You seriously want to try it, too?"

She was already sliding off the bed. "I'll try it," she repeated.

I placed the wheel down on the floor, allowing her to pick it up. She moved to the center of the room where I'd stood and held up the wheel.

Orlando reluctantly picked up the remote once again. "You ready?" he muttered.

Maura nodded, her neck stiff with nerves.

Orlando moved a dial and the rotor returned to life. I chewed hard on the inside of my cheek as the rotor sped up. *Please let it work.* The pessimistic side of me—or rather, the realistic one—told me that it wasn't going to work. That it would be another failed attempt. That Orlando obviously knew his contraption better than my stupid self and...

But then the impossible happened.

As it looked like the blades had reached their maximum speed, Maura's small feet lifted from the floor—not just a fraction of an inch or so, like mine had, but a full three inches. And then the gap widened even more. She was... soaring up to the ceiling!

Orlando looked so utterly shocked by it, he seemed to forget for a moment that he was supposed to be navigating the wheel. As Maura continued gliding upward, he stopped the machine just in time before the blades hit the ceiling. He slowed and lowered them, returning Maura to the floor. He switched off the rotor. And the three of us gaped at each other, hardly daring to believe what had just happened.

"That's..." Orlando stammered. He leapt up from the bed and took the wheel from his sister, examining it with a dumbstruck expression on his face. "I-I can't believe it. I didn't make it for this. I didn't think it would be strong enough—"

My brain lit up with optimism. Like a bright light—light that I had been deprived of for far too long.

I planted a hand on Orlando's shoulder even as he continued to stare down at the device, disbelieving.

"You underestimated your skill, my friend," I said, managing a smile for the first time in—I didn't even know how long. "You created not only an excellent weapon... but a badass flying machine."

Chapter 15: Grace

After experiencing the high that came with discovering that the wheel could fly with Maura, my chest was soon weighed down again as we were faced with the reality of the situation. Yes, we had found out that the wheel could support Maura's weight, but that was only a tiny drop in an ocean of obstacles that now lay ahead of us.

For one thing, how long would the wheel be able to fly with Maura? It was certainly slower moving with her weight, not the nifty thing it had been when I had witnessed it battling with the Bloodless. And how, exactly, would Maura being able to fly help us? The obvious answer was that in the best-case scenario—assuming that the wheel could travel a few miles and would not break down mid-air, and assuming that Maura was willing to risk such a possibility—she would be able to soar with the wheel over the last few streets before the shore, then over the fence itself, and to the other side where Lake Michigan awaited... But then what exactly? We hoped there would be some boats there. Some vessels that were available to hijack.

But Maura would be all alone in this. Orlando and I would be stuck back here. She would have to somehow make her own way, find a phone on her own, and I would have to give her The Shade's numbers to call in case she found a working line. She would have to call up the island and tell them that she was calling on my behalf —and whoever picked up had better believe her. Though I doubted anyone in The Shade would take her words lightly, given that I was missing.

Then there was the danger of Maura being targeted mid-flight. There was certainly no shortage of people to target her with all these hunters and gangs roaming the area. They might even mistake her for me from the ground, since she was a girl. Even if we planned her escape to take place at nighttime, surely someone would notice the weird flying object and Maura's dangling body. Hunters kept watch over this fence, didn't they? As Orlando had suggested before, we would need to locate all the main posts—the main lookouts of the IBSI—and try to pick a spot that was in between these, and a bit more vulnerable.

Maura was looking paler than ever as we discussed all of these potential pitfalls. And I didn't blame her. If she got caught, she wouldn't be in as much hot water as I would be, of course, but I didn't like to think what fate would await her. The IBSI had made it amply clear that all those they had placed in here, they wanted to stay in here. They wanted this part of the city contained, closed off. They might even end Maura for such a transgression as attempted escape.

Orlando was also looking deeply uncomfortable, as uncomfortable as his sister. He would be responsible for using the remote to navigate her over the fence. One wrong move on his part more than likely would prove to be fatal.

After we had talked about everything we could possibly think of that could go wrong, we fell quiet. This was

Maura's life on the line. She had to make the decision whether she was willing to risk it without any pressure from Orlando and me.

We would do all that we could to make this as safe as possible—but even so, there would be nothing even remotely safe about any of it.

Maura leaned back on the mattress and curled up her legs, bringing her knees to her chest. She didn't speak for the next ten minutes. She rocked back and forth, looking rather sick.

Finally she spoke. "I guess we all have to go somehow," she said. She gave her brother a faint, distant smile. "I guess it would be kind of a noble way to go out, wouldn't it? Literally flying for freedom."

Orlando's jaw tightened. He didn't respond.

Maura exhaled. "All right, well... I'm willing to try it."

"Are you sure?" Orlando said, eyeing her seriously.

She slid off the bed and moved to the window, where she stood, gazing out. "I mean, the water looks so close from here. The distance seems so unthreatening. There's hardly any distance to go. If it was further, the decision would probably be a lot harder, but..." She paused her ramblings and was quiet again before concluding, "Yes,

I'm sure."

We joined Maura by the window and looked out at the view afforded us by this high building.

"Do you have any idea where the IBSI's posts are?" I asked.

"Not sure," Orlando said. "We're going to have to try to work it out from a roof."

"But this area in particular is definitely more densely populated," Maura said, glancing to our right. "Oh, look, there's the crematorium. Do you see it? It's just there."

Orlando and I looked toward where she was pointing— a sprawling brick building that looked surprisingly new. Three broad chimneys protruded from the sloping roof, and as I strained my eyes to see, I realized that smoke was coming out of them. It was functioning right now.

"Okay, well, I think we've seen all there is to see from this building," Orlando said. "We need to find somewhere higher. We have to move away from this area without getting caught, and find a taller building." He pointed to our left out of the window. "Further that way, where we've just come from, is definitely quieter."

"Back toward the direction of the church?" I asked.

"Not so far. We need to stay close to the shore,"

Orlando replied.

We gathered our backpacks, and Orlando picked up the blade wheel.

"So our plan should be this," Orlando said quietly as we left the hotel suite and began heading back down the staircase. "We find a tall building and locate a quiet spot where Maura could make the flight. Once we've found it, we try to find a store where I can gather some materials to toughen up the wheel a bit. Make it more suitable for flying."

"I'm not sure that's a good idea, Orlando," Maura said. "Where would we even begin to look? Stores can be the worst places for bumping into trouble. It's where the gangs hang out. Besides, the only mechanical store we know of that hasn't been completely ransacked is all the way on the other side of town. We would have to travel back the way we came."

"There might be another store nearby that we're not aware of," Orlando said. "But you're right. It would mean a delay—possibly a big delay. Plus it would mean wandering about and making it more likely that we get caught... But Maura, I'm worried. Really worried."

"I know," she whispered. "So am I."

The siblings lapsed into silence as we reached the ground floor of the hotel. We moved close to the walls, like shadows, and peered out of the entrance. We couldn't spot any hunters on this road, or anyone else for that matter.

"Let's get out of here while we can," Orlando said. We darted outside and kept close to the walls of the buildings while hurrying along the road. Orlando led us to the end of it and we dove into a cluster of bushes. Here we took a breather, and checked that nobody was following us. They weren't. A good sign.

In the twenty minutes that followed, we moved further away from the area while still maintaining close proximity to the fence and staying parallel to it. Finally, Orlando stopped outside a towering office skyscraper.

"This should definitely be high enough," he said, his eyes panning upward.

Unfortunately, there were more Bloodless in this building. A few too many for comfort. I helped Orlando get rid of them this time. While he tackled a group of ten, coming from our right as we entered the dim lobby, I sent fire blazing at the crowd coming from our left until together we had managed to clear a path deeper into the building.

We had to fell more Bloodless along the way to the top, but finally we reached the roof. We staggered out into the open, back out into the freezing cold. A merciless wind whipped against us, stripping me of any small amount of warmth my body had generated during the climb up here. I sparked a small fire to warm my hands while we scanned the skyline.

"Oh, look," Maura said. "There's the pier."

I could see it now, too, on the other side of the fence. A concrete platform extending into the water, either side of which were small boats. The vessels looked old and neglected. God knew what state they were in, but they were floating at least. Which meant that perhaps they would sail.

"Have you ever navigated a boat before?" I asked Maura.

"Never," she replied.

"Well, you'll have to figure it out somehow," Orlando said, "if you don't find any working communication equipment on board any of the boats. You're going to have to try to get away to find somewhere that does."

Maura nodded stiffly, her lips tightening.

I scanned the area in front of the pier on our side of the electric fence. There were quite a lot of trees in these parts, and also what looked like a small parkland area.

"So," I ventured, "the logical thing would be to navigate Maura over the fence, as directly in line with the pier as possible. Which means having her glide over that greenery."

"Yes," Orlando agreed. It seemed that Orlando and Maura had already come to a firm agreement in their minds not to spend time looking for more mechanical parts to toughen up the wheel. They exchanged glances, before Orlando said, "Now we should wait until dark."

Chapter 16: Grace

The cold was getting to us on the open roof, and it was too dangerous to stay up here for long with helicopters still roaming the skies. So we headed back down into the building. We found somewhere on the top floor to hide out in—a ladies' bathroom, whose windows gave us a good view of the streets surrounding us. Although this area had not been densely filled with hunters when we had arrived, to our disconcertment, more and more figures began to move about the streets as the hours went by.

Aside from the Bloodless and IBSI, there seemed to be

an increasing number of gang members too. Orlando managed to spot Paul Stokes moving along with a crowd of equally threatening-looking men. They looked like toughened brutes through and through, many of them wandering in this cold weather with their chests bare.

We tried to distract ourselves from the filling streets by talking over every single detail of the plan for later that night. Until there was nothing more to discuss on the subject. We all knew what our roles were and what we were supposed to be doing.

Now all that was left was for me to give Maura the phone numbers. I left the bathroom briefly and moved into the office next door where I found a piece of paper and a pen. I wrote down every single number that I had memorized, in case one of them was busy or unavailable. Then, folding up the paper, I returned to the bathroom and handed it to Maura.

"Make sure you take one of the waterproof boxes and stick this in there," I told her. "This whole operation will be for nought if you lose them."

"I know," she said tensely.

She took a few moments to look over the numbers and verify that she could read my handwriting, then cracked open one of the waterproof boxes and stuffed the paper inside. She placed it securely in her backpack.

The sky grew darker as we waited. Though it wasn't all that much of a contrast, given how gloomy the days were here. I glanced out of the window, surprised to see street lights that were on.

"They're not gas lamps, are they?" I asked Orlando.

"Nope. They're electric," Orlando said, also looking surprised. "Seems that this part of the city has kept its flow of electricity. Because of the IBSI's presence, no doubt... I guess that they use electricity to run the crematorium, too."

The crematorium. I couldn't make the large construction out so well from the angle our bathroom window was positioned at, but as I recalled it, I still found the concept strange—the fact that they still kept it working. Why even bother to clear the streets of bodies? Why worry about it? This place was a pit already.

And while I was asking questions, why exactly did they want everybody contained in this area anyway? Maura, Orlando and the other convicts were failed experiments; I didn't understand why the IBSI even cared what happened to them now that they'd finished their testing. Or perhaps they were just containing them because of the government's insistence—since the IBSI had scooped the convicts up from the state's hands, it was their responsibility to ensure that they didn't cause trouble for the rest of society. But then I would have thought that it would have been much simpler just to get rid of them once they proved to no longer be of value. Why bother bringing them here for a slow death?

Hm.

The slamming of a door made all three of us leap from our skins.

It sounded like it was coming from the other end of the hallway, outside the bathroom.

"Oh, no," I breathed. "They're searching the building. They're searching the building!"

Orlando was already rushing to the broken window. He started the blade wheel and navigated it through. Then he grabbed the edges of the pane and, without warning, swung his feet outside. Gripping the remote between his teeth, he lowered his feet to a ledge beneath the bathroom window before he looked up at us with urgency. "Follow me!" he hissed. "We have to hide beneath this ledge."

"Beneath that ledge? Wha—?" I gasped.

"There's another ledge beneath it. Just come!"

Oh, God.

Maura quickly followed her brother while I stared at the two of them, lowering themselves down with an absolutely horrifying drop beneath them. There was nothing attaching them to the building but their bare hands.

My hands were shaking as I grabbed hold of the windowpane and followed their lead, swinging my legs out. I moved further down until I felt the ledge. Then, with blind faith, I lowered myself down further still. I had not been able to see a second ledge, so I just hoped as I reached out my foot...

A hand grabbed my ankle and planted my foot in place on the second, lower ledge. Orlando. *Thank you.* I did all that I possibly could to not look downward as I arrived next to the siblings. If I did steal a glance down, I was sure that I would either have a heart attack or scream.

Orlando navigated the wheel with one hand, round the side of the building. Thank God that thing was quiet. We had to just hope that it would be quiet enough.

We heard voices now, coming from inside the building and drifting through the bathroom window. I gazed upward, experiencing vertigo. At least the first ledge—the one above us—was wide enough to shield us from anyone looking directly downward.

Although I was too afraid to look, there had been hunters beneath us too. If they spotted us out here, then…

I didn't have time to think further about the situation as the door to the bathroom swung open and louder footsteps sounded through the window. The doors of bathroom stalls creaked open and shut. They were searching for me.

Then the footsteps approached the window and I sensed someone's presence just above us. All three of us stopped breathing.

"Anyone in there?" a gruff voice called from the corridor.

There was a pause and then a man replied, in an equally raspy voice, "No."

Slowly, the footsteps moved away from the window and back through the door.

My relief would have been far greater had I not still been perched on this harrowing ledge.

We waited until we could no longer hear any footsteps whatsoever, neither in the bathroom nor in the hallway, before daring to budge. Since I was closest to the window,

I had to begin climbing first. My hands felt numb from the wind and I struggled to gain a grip. I gritted my teeth, willing all the strength that I had left in me to flow to my hands as they wrapped around the upper ledge. I heaved myself upward until I managed to reach out and grasp the window pane. I pulled myself through and went tumbling headfirst into the bathroom. Even as my injured leg connected with the hard bathroom floor, I barely felt it. I was too relieved to be back on solid ground. Maura and Orlando piled in through the window after me before he brought in the wheel.

After verifying that the men had indeed left our floor, we shut ourselves again in the bathroom and slumped down against the wall, breathing deeply.

At least there was one good thing that came with that scare. Whoever had been here—hunters or criminals, we had no way of knowing—had searched this room now, so hopefully they wouldn't bother to come searching it again anytime soon. Hopefully, we would be safe here at least for the next few hours, until the streets were emptier and we were able to risk Maura beginning her flight.

Chapter 17: Grace

As the night wore on, I was beginning to fear that the streets might never empty—these roads surrounding us which previously had been fairly quiet had become busy with inmates and hunters. But when the early morning hours drew in, finally, the area became less populated. Not empty, for sure—but emptier. Which would have to be good enough for us.

Because we couldn't wait much longer—after all, morning would arrive in a few hours and it would start getting lighter. It was now or never. And Maura had realized it as she gazed nervously out of the window.

The siblings met each other's eyes, and they nodded in silent understanding.

"I should go now," Maura said quietly.

Wordlessly, Orlando stooped to pick up his wheel. He handed it to her. "Let's just check that it's working okay first," he murmured.

After donning her gas-mask helmet, Maura gripped the wheel and raised it above her head. Once she had indicated to her brother that she was ready, he nudged the remote and the blades began to spin. He put it on full speed, and thankfully, it still worked—it managed to lift her off the ground, however slowly. She looked strained as she clung on, rising higher and higher toward the ceiling. Orlando made the wheel hover for a while, still testing its endurance.

Then he lowered it, returning Maura's feet to the floor.

"So, it's still working," he said to her. "Are you ready?"

"I'll never be more ready," she replied.

"Right."

Maura moved forward, closer to Orlando, and wrapped her arms around him. She buried her head against his chest while he hugged her back. I stepped away and turned my back on them to look out of the window and allow them at least some semblance of privacy.

It was hard to imagine what Orlando must have been feeling in that moment. I didn't have any siblings, but the thought of being responsible for anybody embarking on this crazy flight was enough to give me chills, let alone someone as close to me as my own sister.

"We are going to do this," Orlando said. "And we're going to succeed. *You're* going to succeed." He spoke firmly, though his uneven tone of voice betrayed his doubt. "You're going to reach the other side of the fence. And then you're going to find a phone. And all three of us are going to get out of here."

Maura arrived next to me, her fingers curving around the window sill.

Orlando approached with the blade wheel. He handed it to her again. Luckily, the window was wide enough to hold the diameter of the contraption, which would definitely make takeoff easier. Maura stood with her feet apart, the wheel raised over her head.

Orlando and I stepped back.

It was hard to believe that the moment had finally arrived. But for the sake of all of our sanity, it was a moment that we could not prolong.

Maura realized this. She nodded a final time to her brother and tightened her grip on the wheel's handles.

Orlando started up the rotor, which began to spin and lift her into the air. She hovered upward until her feet were level with the window sill. And then Orlando moved her outward... Outward, outward, away from the safety of the bathroom floor, and over the hair-raising drop of more than a dozen stories.

If only she could have zip lined this distance instead.

I dared not even budge an inch from my spot, lest it distract Orlando. He looked like he had broken out into a sudden, heavy sweat, as perspiration dripped from his forehead. His eyes were so intensely fixed on the remote and his sister that they bulged in their sockets.

I could no longer make out Maura's expression clearly as she moved deeper into the darkness of the night. Though I could imagine the terror flashing in her eyes. Thankfully, the wind was no longer strong, and I realized that it had even stopped raining.

All good omens.

Now we just need to continue this lucky streak.

She'll make it to the other side. She will. I know it.

I tried to cram my head with as many positive thoughts

as I possibly could to drown out the fear eating away at me.

I scanned the streets that she was directly above now for signs of movement. There was nobody, at least not in the stretch that she was soaring over. Slowly but steadily, she crossed all of the roads and reached the green area, moving closer to the trees.

Hold on, Maura. Keep holding on. You're doing a good job. Her hands and arms must have been aching by now. I wished that I could call out to her, that Orlando could— that we could both try to comfort her, assure her somehow—but she was on her own.

I watched with bated breath as Orlando navigated the wheel over the trees. "You're doing well, Orlando," I whispered. "You're doing well…"

"I'm worried about the fence," he croaked.

"What do you mean?" I asked.

"I just had a thought," he replied. "What if it sends some kind of… energy upward? Some kind of forcefield?"

I frowned. Unless a witch had done something to the fence, I figured that Orlando was just overthinking things because of his nerves. It struck me as just a normal electric fence—like the one I had escaped over back in IBSI's base on the other side of the river.

"Just keep going," I encouraged him. "She's almost there…"

My voice drained away as a bloodcurdling screech lit up the night. A potential forcefield above the fence had suddenly become the very least of our worries.

I didn't often swear—it wasn't something my parents had ever approved of. But on catching sight of a giant figure zooming through the sky from our right, a slew of curses escaped my lips.

A mutant. I had been so preoccupied by all the other damn obstacles we were surrounded by—the IBSI, inmates and Bloodless—that I had forgotten all about the hunters' mutants. Besides, I hadn't seen a single one since I'd been in this part of the city. It hadn't even occurred to me that the IBSI could have them patrolling the night skies.

Everything that happened next was a blur of panic and confusion. Even though we'd both heard the screeching at the same time, Orlando had spotted it later than I had— being forced to keep his concentration on Maura. But now that he stole a glance at the monster, he cursed louder than I had.

I wasn't sure what he tried to do next as he began moving the remote's dials frantically. Pull Maura back toward us? Urge her onward, crossing the final stretch before the lake? I would never find out. The mutant was too quick. With supernatural speed it slammed into Maura, deftly avoiding the blades, and scooped her up in its talons. Letting go of the wheel, Maura shrieked and flailed, but there was nothing she could do. There was nothing any of us could do as the mutant beat its wings ferociously, turning in the sky, and launched toward the opposite direction—back toward the densely populated IBSI area.

Orlando couldn't send the blade wheel after the creature in case he ended up injuring Maura. And even if he only managed to damage the mutant with the knives, he still risked Maura's demise—if the thing dropped her from this height, I doubted she had any chance of surviving.

The two of us gaped as the mutant soared off with the girl. But then Orlando snapped out of his stupor. He called the wheel back to us—it was ten times faster now that it no longer carried Maura's weight—and grabbed it as it came flying through the window. Then, without a backward glance, he darted out of the bathroom and into the corridor. I sprinted after him as he raced to the staircase and we both rushed down the stairs. It was a small mercy that no Bloodless slowed our journey to the ground level. We leapt the last of the stairs leading to the lobby and dashed to the exit. Orlando, in his panic and blind desperation, barely even looked around the street to check that it was empty before lurching out. I could only be a little more cautious in my attempt to keep up with him— I donned my gas-mask helmet before hurtling onto the sidewalk.

Orlando's eyes were on the sky. We could still see the mutant in the distance.

"Where do you think it could be taking her?" I gasped. It looked like it was heading toward… the crematorium.

Orlando did not answer. He was in too much of a daze. His focus remained fixed on the sky as we roamed through the streets, getting dangerously closer to the hubbub of hunter activity. *Crap.* I could hardly ask Orlando to slow down and think when his sister was in such mortal danger. But heck, this wasn't a good idea. If we got in trouble too, there would be no chance of helping her. Besides, if the mutant had wanted to kill Maura, eat or rip into her, surely it would've just done that already in the sky? It seemed to be taking her somewhere, which indicated that it meant to keep her alive, at least for the time being.

As much as it killed me to do it, I reached out and grabbed Orlando's arm. "Wait," I gasped, struggling to pull him to a stop. "Wait," I repeated. "We need to think this through. Just running ahead blindly isn't going to help get your sister back!"

He shoved me aside, ignoring my words as if I had not spoken, and continued in his race. And again, I had no choice but to follow him.

He only slowed down as we reached the end of the road because he was forced to. We found ourselves face to face with a group of men turning a corner—a gang of criminals with shaven heads, tattered clothes and weapons. Lots of weapons. Knives and guns stuck out from their belts and protruded beneath their garments. I could only assume, on hearing the commotion—Maura's screaming and then Orlando's and my yelling—they had come running.

I thanked God that I'd had the sense to put my gas mask on before venturing out here. At least they couldn't recognize me instantly.

Orlando, on the other hand, was not wearing his, but he wasn't a wanted person around here.

Orlando moved to dodge them, slip by the sidewalk on the opposite side of the road, but they quickly hurried toward him. They pulled out guns and pointed them at Orlando, forcing him to a stop, while I found myself backing away from four intimidating men moving toward me. At the lead was Paul Stokes. I could make out his features more clearly now that he was so close. He was a muscled man with cropped hair—like everyone in this place seemed to have, be they men or women—and a wide scar that stretched from his right eye down to his jawline.

Since I was dressed pretty bulkily—wearing not only my helmet but also my waterproof overalls—and since my long hair was tucked away, it was possible that he couldn't even tell my gender yet. And I had to keep it that way.

The mutant had flown out of sight by now, Maura's screams fading into the distance. But all Orlando and I had to think about now was getting away from these men. Far away.

"Reveal yourself!" Paul demanded of me.

I looked anxiously toward Orlando. My instinct was to bolt right now, but I couldn't just leave him. I was also torn as to how, exactly, I ought to defend myself. The easiest way would've been to make use of my fire powers, but that would be a dead giveaway. The IBSI knew about my powers by now—they had witnessed them enough back in their base. They had probably already described me to this gang.

They would instantly know who I was, and any onlookers who arrived at all the noise and disruption a battle would cause would also know.

Orlando's finger twitched over the wheel's remote. Fear gripped me for him. One wrong move, and they'd shoot him.

"Put the wheel down," one of the men shouted at him, "along with every other weapon you're carrying."

Oh, God. Where are those damn Bloodless when you need them? Some of those nasty creatures causing a distraction here would really be useful about now.

Orlando didn't budge. He stared back at them defiantly, his jaw twitching. "Let me pass." He spoke up in a voice that was surprisingly level. "I'm of no interest to you."

The men glanced at me, me and my hidden face.

Paul cocked his gun and raised it to me. "Remove your mask," he commanded me again. "I will not ask you a third time."

In the split second that every one of the criminals looked at me, Orlando made his move. He dropped the wheel and pressed down hard on his controls. The rotor roared to life and went slashing toward the men.

Then came a gunshot. The men hadn't been distracted by me long enough.

The blade wheel stopped spinning and crashed to the waterlogged ground. Orlando staggered back, dropping the remote.

I couldn't stop myself from yelling out to him—which instantly gave away my gender.

I hadn't seen exactly through this gloom where one of them had shot him, or which one exactly, but Orlando clutched his shoulder with one hand. He let out a deep groan, his face contorting in agony.

No. No!

Paul lurched for me while the other men crowded around Orlando.

There was no time for games anymore.

Pulling the lighter from my pocket, I sparked it and blazed a fire in my palms. Paul leapt back. The IBSI should have warned him of my powers, but he still looked alarmed. *Never met a fae before, huh?* I made the flames billow toward him, forcing him to dart backward to avoid being scorched to a crisp.

The men who'd been closing in on Orlando whirled around, their focus on me, Orlando momentarily forgotten.

Gripping my mask, I pulled it from my head and threw it to the ground, revealing my face. My loose hair flailed wildly in the breeze as I glowered at each of them.

My only objective right now was to distract them from Orlando. I was already foreseeing them ending him. Kicking him to the ground and lodging bullets into him until he released his final breath. These people saw no value in other people's lives.

Except mine.

They did value mine.

They would not shoot at me now that they had seen who I was—I was sure of that. The IBSI didn't want me dead yet, at least not until they had reclaimed and interrogated me. I knew that much from my previous experience of being their prisoner.

I was the key to these inmates' freedom. They needed me alive.

"As my friend said," I called to the men, "he is of no

interest to you. I, however, *am*…" My fingers cradled my lighter as I narrowed my eyes on them. Dropping my voice to a menacing tone, I dared, "Come and get me."

Chapter 18: Grace

My confident tone did not mirror my inner state of being. My gut was churning with nerves as I dashed off down the street in the opposite direction from Orlando. The men's footsteps hammered against the road as they raced after me.

I had to get as far away as I possibly could, and hopefully Orlando would have the strength to keep going alone. Though going where, exactly, I had no clue. How would he ever reclaim his sister? How would any of us ever escape from here now? Maura had become our only hope of crossing to the other side of the fence. Of reaching a phone.

But I no longer had time to think as I accidentally turned into a narrow alleyway that, to my horror, turned out to be a dead end.

The criminals came rushing after me and I quickly hurried to a narrow staircase that wound up the side of one building's wall. I scaled it as fast as my legs could carry me.

Bloodless, oh, Bloodless… Where are you?

I needed to find a crowd of them. With my fire, it would be much easier for me to evade the monsters than for these criminals—especially since the Bloodless should be more drawn to their blood than to a half-fae's.

I would have smiled bitterly at the sheer irony if I hadn't been in such a frenzy to escape. I'd spent practically every waking moment since I arrived in this city fearing bumping into the nightmarish creatures, and now that I needed them, I couldn't find them anywhere. *Typical. Just typical.*

I had to keep moving. Reaching the top of the roof, I lunged for a door that led back down through the interior building. Forcing the stiff door open, I hurried into the building and down the internal staircase. I blazed back fire over my shoulder every so often to keep them at a safe distance until I arrived on the ground floor. Here I could continue running and searching for Bloodless. I had to find the monsters before the IBSI came to assist the criminals in the chase. Once they did that, things would escalate to a whole new level.

My heart was in my throat as my feet pounded against the concrete, splashing through deep puddles. I barely had time to look where I was going as I darted through the streets.

And then, I saw it. A sight both beautiful and terrifying. A group of Bloodless hulking at the end of the road I'd just turned into.

"Hey, you guys!" I bellowed toward them. I was sure that they had never been addressed as such in the whole of their Bloodless lives. They stopped in their tracks and spun around. Then, as hard as my pulse raced, I went darting toward them. The Bloodless welcomed my advance eagerly.

I cast a glance over my shoulder to see the men had already turned around and started darting in the opposite direction on spotting the crowd of Bloodless. I blazed up a fire just in time to prevent the Bloodless from diving straight into me, and manipulated the flames to encourage them in the direction of the criminals. The monsters were not slow to take the cue—they immediately ran after the men.

I watched as they fled and breathed a sigh of relief. Relief that didn't last long as I thought of Orlando. If they were heading in his direction, with his injury, I didn't know how quick he'd be to defend himself. I had to get back to him. The thought of losing him now in this time of deepest desperation sent despair rippling through my chest.

I took a right down a side alley that appeared to run exactly parallel to the main road. There had to be an opening here... somewhere I could turn left to rejoin it and...

I yelped as I turned the alley's corner and collided with three men. The collision was so forceful, I was knocked from my feet and fell forward into a puddle. I barely had time to swivel around and verify who I had just collided with before hands pinned my legs down. A heavy weight dropped against my back, flattening me against the wet concrete. Another pair of hands closed around my wrists, forcing my palms to the ground and into the deep puddle I had tripped into.

I screamed, managing to twist my head round just enough to realize who was on top of me. Paul. He and the two other men must've taken a detour the moment they saw the Bloodless and wound their way here through the back alleys.

No!

I tried to free my hands, raise them from the puddle, but two heavy booted feet ran in front of me and pressed down hard against them, keeping them firmly where they were, deep in the water. I had lost the spark in my hands and now I couldn't reignite it. Even if I manipulated the water to leave the puddle, I needed to reach my lighter.

Another pair of hands pressed down over my wrists before Paul's hands slipped away. Instead he slid them down my body. One by one, he removed the weapons from my person—a gun and my stash of lighters. I heard what sounded like the drawing of a blade from its sheath, and then the slicing of fabric. My backpack came loose. He lifted it off me and threw it aside before continuing to roam my body with his hands—far more intrusively than was required.

"Get off me!" I wheezed.

Paul slammed my head down into the puddle, causing

me to choke on the muddy water. His hands continued their unnecessary wandering until even one of his companions remarked, "Come on, man. That's enough."

Paul's weight remained on me, but at least his hands stopped moving.

"We need to get her to Martin," he muttered to the other two. "He's got the sedatives. Should have ripped some off him before we parted, dammit."

"What about the others?" one of the men asked.

"What do you mean, Tim?" Paul responded.

"We need to wait for them," Tim said. "Obviously. So we all get out together."

"No. We're not going to wait around," Paul replied. "If they find us on the way back, that's all well and good. They can join the group and we can tell the IBSI that they assisted. But if not, then it's tough."

"Wait a second, Stokes." The other man spoke—the man who was standing on my hands. "Jade is with the others. I can't leave her behind."

"Then go look for her," Paul replied coldly. "You know the route I'll take. Go find her and reach us in time so you can join us. I doubt I'll be moving that fast, anyway, with this little lady flailing about…Though I suggest she doesn't." He gripped the back of my neck threateningly.

"You're going to screw over a lot of people, you know that," the third man said. "We all came—"

"You know that you guys have just been lied to anyway." I spoke up suddenly, interrupting their quickly heating conversation. "There isn't actually any treatment or freedom planned for you. It's all a lie."

"Shut your mouth unless you're asked to open it," Paul snapped, tugging painfully at my hair.

"You're just being used, Paul," I went on, gritting my teeth against the pain. "You're being used like a pawn. You're just too dumb to see it."

He craned my neck back again painfully and hissed, "I told you to shut it."

"The truth hurts," I managed, "I know."

"What truth?" Tim asked.

"Don't start encouraging her!" Paul snarled.

"I wanna hear what she has to say," Tim replied.

I wasn't sure why Tim was so eager to have me speak, honestly. Perhaps because he too was having doubts about the IBSI's promises.

Paul growled impatiently, but released my neck, allowing me to breathe normally. Truth be told, I wasn't sure what I was doing or even saying. I had to wrangle some way to keep them distracted, because once they got hold of sedatives, it would be the beginning of the end for me. I would find myself waking up back in the IBSI's headquarters, and this time I would never see the light of day again.

"What is it that we are ignorant of, then?" Paul snapped.

As I stumbled for words, something occurred to me. The IBSI should have no reason to know about my ability to manipulate water. As far as we knew, they still knew very little about fae. Indeed, many of them had been surprised when I had blazed fire in my palms back in their headquarters. I was almost positive that these criminals wouldn't know about my water powers either. If Tim would just stop clamping down my wrists with his boots, and if I could just sit at the right angle… I was surrounded by wide, deep puddles that filled the dips in the dilapidated road. More like mini-paddling pools.

"I'll tell you if you let me sit up," I said. "You're killing my hands."

Paul coughed out a dry laugh. "You seriously think we're stupid, don't you?"

"Why, yes," I admitted. "As I said already, I do think

you're stupid. Downright moronic, in fact, for believing what the IBSI told you."

Paul moved to hurt me again but Tim got in his way.

"We've confiscated the matches and lighters, and you searched her." Tim addressed Paul. "She has no way to spark up a fire." I heard the clicking of a gun, then I felt a barrel press against the back of my neck. I reminded myself again that they couldn't kill me. If they did, they would risk ruining their chances of treatment and release.

"I'm holding a gun," Tim informed me, like I hadn't already noticed. "One wrong move, and it's goodbye to you, sweetie."

I nodded.

Slowly, Tim's boots lifted from my wrists. I drew my hands toward me and cradled them to my chest. Pain shot through my wrists and arms as I tried to move my fingers. My pinky wouldn't move at all. I was sure that Tim had broken it.

I sat upright gradually, taking my time so as to not cause them alarm. Now I could face the men properly. Paul remained right next to me, barely a foot away, his eyes digging into mine, while Tim remained standing with the other man—both of whom were now pointing guns at me.

I dropped my hands discreetly into the water.

"Now you have a minute to tell us your secret before we leave," Paul said. "So you'd better hurry up."

I drew in a breath even as I gained a feel for the puddle water. "Well," I began, wetting my lower lip thoughtfully, "it's kind of a conspiracy they've got going on. And the reason you're all here has to do with why they want me in the first place. I know something that could bring this whole operation down. I know the secret of why you're here—" As I babbled non-information, I tried to estimate how many liters of water were within my proximity. More than four hundred, I was sure. I only needed a few seconds of distraction. My backpack lay only a few feet away...

I continued to beat around the bush with the men, dragging out revealing what the actual "secret" was, until finally, as I sensed that Paul was on the verge of just grabbing me and escorting me to whoever Martin was, I gathered the courage to make my move. I caused all the surrounding water to burst up at once. A thick wall of water crashed into the men and smacked them in the face, causing the guns to drop from their hands as they staggered back.

Not missing a beat, I hurled myself toward my backpack

and shot a hand inside to rummage for one of my spare lighters. But the lighters had been removed. Heck, there weren't even any matchboxes left. One of the guys must have emptied it and taken them for themselves, stuffed them into one of their own backpacks, while I'd been face down on the concrete. My hand, however, did brush against a gun.

The shock of my mini-tsunami wore off quickly. As Tim and the other man, who still remained nameless to me, leapt for the guns they had dropped and Paul reached for a gun in his belt, I already knew what was going to happen next. They were going to take me down however they could. Shoot me in the legs. Paralyze me, so they could escort me to my doom.

My brain numb with panic, I did the only thing that I could think to do. I slid out the gun in my hands from the backpack and started firing at all three men in rapid succession. None of them could respond fast enough. And a few moments later, all three of them collapsed. Motionless.

I stopped breathing as I stared at the three men. The three... bodies. *No.* I hadn't meant to kill them. I really hadn't. I'd only meant to hurt them, paralyze them before they could paralyze me.

But, although I'd used a gun before in training, I had never used it before in real combat. And in my moment of panic, I hadn't been aiming the way I'd been taught to aim. Raw survival instinct had clouded my judgment and I'd just... fired. Fired. Fired. Anywhere and everywhere.

The gun slipped from my trembling hands as I approached the bodies.

Three lives. I'd just claimed three lives.

It took several moments of gazing at the men for the reality to sink in. As I realized what I'd done. What I was now.

My innocence was lost.

I'd become a murderer. Just like them.

CHAPTER 19: BEN

To my surprise, the tracker that Shayla had given Corrine to locate Arwen and her accompanying witches led us to the outskirts of the IBSI's base in Chicago. We spotted the witches lurking near the headquarters' borders, talking with one another behind a large cluster of bushes. Corrine immediately hurtled toward her daughter and gripped her by the shoulders.

"Arwen!" she hissed.

The young witch's eyes bulged in alarm to see her mother.

"Mom," she gasped.

"What in the name of The Sanctuary were you thinking in taking Grace to Hawaii?" Corrine shook her none too gently. "You betrayed me, and you betrayed your father. We trusted you with the security of our island! You went and abused your privileges in the worst—"

"What's happening?" I demanded, cutting through Corrine's chastisement. She would have ample time for that later, no doubt. "Where is my daughter? You think she's here?"

Arwen, glassy-eyed and red-cheeked, tore her gaze away from her mother and fixed it on me. "Yes," she murmured.

"What makes you think that?"

"We went to Hawaii first. Breached their base and set off their alarms in the process, but we managed to extract information from one of the workers in the air base they have there. We asked him for a recent list of destinations and he told us there had only been one flight that day—a chopper chartered for Chicago."

Right. I grimaced, turning my eyes on the high, electrified fences. I turned to Lucas and Kailyn, who were looking at me, waiting for my go-ahead. I nodded. "Let's go inside."

We thinned ourselves and sank through the fence,

emerging on the other side in a small courtyard. We moved into the nearest building and found ourselves inside a reception area.

Now think. If Grace is really in this place, where would they have taken her?

I spotted a wide map display fixed to the wall near the reception desk. We moved to it and examined it. I scanned past the residential area which seemed to occupy the first five buildings of the compound, and stopped on a building marked "Laboratories". The hunters could have brought my daughter here to experiment on her. She was a fae, after all. And fae were creatures the IBSI still knew very little about, for they rarely had the opportunity to encounter one, much less catch one. Grace, being only half fae and unable to thin herself in order to escape, would be the perfect test subject. They could be performing experiments on her right at this moment, perhaps even taking something from her, just as I suspected they had taken something from River...

Even after all these years, we still weren't sure what exactly the IBSI had done to my wife—though I suspected they'd collected a sample of her eggs. I suspected that they had been used to lay the foundation stones of their drug development today. Since River had been half supernatural, and they were also essentially attempting to become half supernatural with whatever concoction they were brewing up for their men, perhaps her DNA had come in useful in their preliminary research. I could only speculate about what they'd done to River, but I didn't even want to consider what they might do to Grace.

"So where do we go?" Kailyn asked beneath her breath.

My eyes passed the laboratory and continued roaming the map. Then something else caught my eye—an area located on the fifth floor of the building about six blocks away from us, entitled "Interrogation Quarters."

I shuddered to think that my Grace could have been taken there too. "Okay," I breathed. "Let's search the lab first, and if we don't find her there, we'll head to the Interrogation Quarters. We should stick together and not wander off," I added, mostly to my uncle. He had a habit of taking detours at the most inconvenient of times. I was sure that it was subconscious; he just didn't like to be put in a straitjacket or follow a rigid path.

We zoomed through the headquarters and reached the lab. It was enormous, consisting of numerous floors and departments. We searched the entirety of it, but did not find my daughter. I wasn't sure whether to be relieved or disappointed about that. Next, we headed to the interrogation area, which consisted of fifteen different rooms containing tinted glass windows. All were completely empty.

I drew in a breath, hoping that Arwen had not been lied to by the guy she had questioned back in Hawaii. I hated to consider the possibility that Grace might not even be here, but somewhere else entirely. Somewhere completely unknown.

"We need to consult a map again," I said. I began leading us back to the reception but along the way, we came across another map in one of the hallways.

"Hmm," I murmured, scanning the compound.

"What about the Restricted Access building?" Lucas suggested.

I frowned. Restricted Access. Where was that? *Ah, yes.* I spotted it. Right on the other side of the compound—on the top floor of the very last building, it seemed.

"Let's go there, then," I said.

As we hurried toward the back of the compound, I had no idea what to expect. Maybe some kind of secret lab, where they developed their most confidential drugs, that wasn't open to just any old IBSI member?

To my surprise, the Restricted Access floor of the final building appeared to be a residential area. We found ourselves arriving at the end of a long red-carpeted hallway that resembled a hotel's. The lighting was warm and inviting, and there were oil paintings on the walls. On either side of us were dark mahogany wood doors... and there were names engraved on each one. Maybe these were apartments where all the HQ's big shots resided. Because there were many other apartment blocks that we had already passed, closer to the entrance of the compound, that had not been restricted access.

We passed the first door on our right —"Oliver Hyatt" was the name etched on the front of it. I had never heard of the name. The door on our left was engraved with yet another unknown name. We passed by three more doors, upon which were marked more meaningless names, until we reached the seventh and final door along this end of the corridor.

"Atticus Conway" was the name on this one.

Atticus Conway. I froze. That wasn't exactly a common name. That... that was Lawrence's father? The same man who had come to The Shade to reclaim him. The same man who had sworn that he had no connection whatsoever with the IBSI. My pulse raced, doubts and suspicions crowding my mind. If this was him, and he had an apartment up here in the restricted access area, he was obviously some kind of leader. *Could he have something to do with my daughter being brought here?*

I took a deep breath before stepping through Atticus' closed door with Lucas and Kailyn.

We emerged in an apartment that looked like it belonged in a five-star hotel. No expense had been spared in its furnishings and decor, and it was immaculately clean. The marble-floor of the foyer we had just stepped into looked fit to eat a meal off of.

As we moved deeper into the apartment, we looked left and right, gazing into the spacious rooms. And then I heard a voice. A muffled voice, coming from somewhere in the back of the apartment. We hurried forward, spilling through several closed doorways. We moved through a dining room and a sitting room before arriving in a room lined with towering bookcases. A library. But the voice was coming from deeper still in the apartment. Perhaps there was a hidden doorway in this library somewhere, but it didn't matter to us because we could pass through walls.

We sank into a shelf of books, through the concrete wall, and when we appeared on the other side, we were in an office.

And there sat Atticus—in front of a luxuriously wide wooden desk, sitting upright in a swivel chair, a phone pressed to his right ear. From where we stood, we could only see the back of his dusty blonde hair. He wore a light black pullover, thin enough for us to see the muscles in his back tensing as he leaned on the edge of his seat.

"Yes, I know, Brian," he was saying, his voice as tight as his posture. "But that doesn't change anything. We have to know for sure." He paused, listening impatiently to whoever Brian was on the other end of the phone. He exhaled. "Yes. We have the copy—but dammit, did you not read the note? There are obviously other backups."

Note? Backups?

I moved closer and realized that his broad frame had been blocking a laptop from our view. The computer sat in front of him on the desk. I gazed over his shoulder at the screen. A page with a black background was pulled up, filled with mostly tiny white text. As my eyes roamed the omnibar at the top of the browser, the page was some kind of local file on his computer, rather than online.

At the top of the page was a title—the largest font on the page—in bold white letters:

"Fight for Open Education on the Bloodless Antidote."

I gaped at the words.

Bloodless antidote?

What?

There's an antidote?

In all our witches' and jinn's years of trying, they'd never been able to find a cure for the Bloodless infection. Had these hunters found one? If they had, then this would be one of the rare occurrences in history that science had trumped magic.

I moved closer to the screen to read the tiny text further down the page, but Brian must have said something inflammatory on the other end of the phone to Atticus. Just as I made the attempt, Atticus slammed the laptop shut before I could even make out the first sentence.

"No!" he insisted. "No. No. No. We don't have that sort of time. I have already sent troops out to look for the girl. Yes, yes, they searched the river already. No, she wasn't there. Her body was nowhere for miles. She must have climbed out and now she's out there somewhere. We'll find her soon enough but, look, this isn't relevant to what you are supposed to be doing for me. You need to…"

Atticus' voice trailed off in my brain as I remained fixed on fragments of the previous sentences he had spoken.

"Already sent troops out to look for the girl. Climbed out. Out there somewhere."

That had to be my Grace. She'd found a way to escape. I couldn't help but feel a swell of pride, even as my mind surged with worry. *Where somewhere? What river?*

As much as I was burning to know what the heck I had just read on that webpage, my fatherly instinct simply wouldn't allow me to stand still here a moment longer. Lucas and Kailyn understood my intention. The three of us immediately raced out of the office, into the library and back through the apartment.

Returning to the corridor outside, I whispered to my companions, "The river. We need to locate the river."

Chapter 20: Grace

Run, Grace. Run.

I couldn't stay here any longer. I had to move. I had to get somewhere safe, where I wouldn't be found. But I had to find Orlando too.

Taking in the harrowing sight of my own doing one last time—the three men lying dead in pools of their own blood—I grabbed the backpack they had confiscated from me, along with one of theirs. After verifying that it contained a lighter, I headed off down the alleyway. I sparked up a flame in my palms, hoping to draw comfort from its familiar warmth. But I was still shaking, shaking as though I was freezing cold.

What could I have done differently? I wondered to myself as I hurried down the street. I had done what I could in my situation. I had done what I could to survive. And yet—*Isn't that what many murderers tell themselves?*

But I couldn't allow my mind to get bogged down with such futile thoughts now. I had done what I had done. And now I had to fight to stay alert if I wanted to stand any chance of pulling through this nightmare alive.

The alleyway wound left abruptly, leading me right back to the main street where we had first stumbled into trouble with the gang. It had been abandoned now, likely due to the Bloodless sweeping down it—the criminals who had been on my tail had either been killed, turned, or fled for safety. But once the IBSI got wind from one of the escaped criminals that I had been located, this road would become a whole lot more crowded.

Where is Orlando?

He had still been standing at the end of this road when I had last seen him. He had been injured, but standing. Would he have continued onward to find his sister? *Dammit. Where is he now?*

As I arrived at the end of the road, the exact spot where

we had been stopped by the criminals, I gazed down at the ground and spotted Orlando's blood where he had been standing. The blood trailed to my right, taking a turn at the end of the road. Christ, he had been bleeding a lot. The drips led me down a boulevard—all the way along it—and when I reached the end, to my surprise, the drips wound right again. If he had been trying to follow Maura's direction, he should've turned left. Right… that was back toward where I had run.

Had he meant to come after me to help me? Why else would he have turned this way? Unless he had become delirious from the blood loss and lost his sense of direction. His blood trail led me down yet another road and then into another maze of alleyways until it stopped at the foot of a wide trashcan, leaning against a tall building. Venturing around its corner, I gasped as I caught sight of Orlando, collapsed in a heap. His eyes were closed, his upper right arm still bleeding freely. He had carried the wheel all this way; it lay a few feet away from him, along with the abandoned remote.

I dropped down to him and felt his pulse. He was alive, at least, though his breathing was shallow and uneven. It sank in how insanely lucky he was that Bloodless had not yet followed his trail of blood and smoked him out. That could still happen at any moment, of course.

I dove into my backpack and pulled out the spare set of pants the siblings had packed for me. I wrapped it tightly around his wound, attempting with all my might to stem the blood flow. Then I summoned water from a nearby puddle and splashed it against his face.

His eyelids moved, and he drew in a sharp, wincing breath.

Yes, come on, Orlando. Come on.

I dove into my backpack again and withdrew a bottle of water. I cracked it open and held it to his lips, coaxing him to drink. His dry lips parted, and he allowed the bottle between his teeth. He drank slowly, apparently in pain each time he swallowed, but he managed to down half of it.

"It's okay," I croaked, trying to comfort myself as much as him. "I've got you. You're going to be okay."

As his vision focused, he cursed. "Dammit, Grace," he wheezed. "What happened to you? I tried to come after you—"

My breath hitched. "You shouldn't have tried," I whispered. "You shouldn't have." But I understood why he had. He was just as alone now as I was. He needed me as much as I needed him.

I glanced up and down the alley nervously, expecting to see a surge of Bloodless come streaming down toward us at any moment. I wound one arm around his waist and tugged him upward. "Come on," I said, trying to be gentle but needing to be urgent at the same time. "We can't sit around here."

"You're right," he managed. "We have to keep moving. I'm sure that monster was carrying her toward the crematorium. We need to head there."

I clenched my fists nervously. That was not what I was going to suggest. I didn't know what to do now in our situation other than to find yet another shelter, somewhere we could go to take a short breather and recover our thoughts. But I couldn't expect Orlando to be able to sit still when his sister had been carried off. If I'd had a sister, I would be the same way.

"Okay," I whispered. "So we have to head to the crematorium. There are tall buildings near there, right?" I asked, straining to remember the sight I had glimpsed from the bathroom we had been holed up in in our previous shelter.

"Yeah," he said.

Then at least we could get a peek inside the compound. There didn't seem to be any windows in the actual building, but there had been grounds around it. Though I found it hard to believe the mutant would just be hanging around outside with Maura.

But there was nowhere else Orlando would head right now.

"So it's nearby," I said.

"Only a few blocks away from here, I think," he replied.

And we had to hope like hell that the criminals who had spied my identity before being chased off by the Bloodless had not yet had a chance to reach their nearest IBSI scout.

I collected Orlando's blade wheel along with his remote before helping him to his feet. He was awfully weak. I fed him some more water. At least he was coping better than a regular human would. Maybe whatever illness the IBSI had given him had affected his system somehow, made him tougher in some ways, even though he looked like a sickly thing.

I pulled Orlando as fast as he could move through the streets, stopping every time we reached a doorway to back up against it and look left and right, to check that nobody was following us.

I was relieved when Orlando informed me that we were close enough to the crematorium to enter one of the buildings. We entered a three-story restaurant. As we moved through it, the place was hardly recognizable as such, with all its tables and chairs splintered and strewn about the floor—its once beautiful decor slashed and faded.

We moved to the third floor and crossed to the other side of the building where, I realized, we had an extremely good view of the crematorium. We were shockingly close. Just a street's width away.

"These buildings directly around the crematorium," Orlando said, gesturing to the room around us, "are forbidden, apparently. If we got caught in here by the IBSI, we'd be put to death."

I stared at him, though not disbelievingly. *Thanks for telling me that before we climbed up here.*

Though I was as good as dead anyway, wherever the IBSI found me.

We gazed over the wall enclosing the crematorium to see a small outside area, which consisted primarily of a parking lot. It was home to several large black tanks—

signature IBSI style.

There was no soul in sight though. No sign of the mutant. No sign of Maura. No sign of anything but the monstrous vehicles.

My eyes roamed the vast, grim structure. *So they sweep the fallen bodies from the roads in those tanks every so often and bring them to the crematorium.* I took in the high, wide chimneys spiking up from the roof of the main building. They were still smoking, even now.

Even though I was sure that it was the last thing on Orlando's mind, I couldn't help but ask, "Did they, like, do a sweep recently? The IBSI? Those chimneys have been smoking ever since we arrived in this area."

Orlando shrugged, his eyes wide and filled with angst as he scanned the parking lot.

"Maybe I was mistaken," he rasped. "Maybe the mutant took Maura somewhere else." He glanced beyond the crematorium, further to our right up the road. "Maybe there's an IBSI post up there, where she was taken."

Or she could already be inside *the crematorium…* That was a suggestion I figured I ought to keep to myself.

Silence fell between us. And I was certain that the same question was running through both of our minds. *What now?*

We had lost Maura's trail. Would Orlando want to risk venturing inside the crematorium to look for her when she could've gone somewhere else entirely? Where would we even start looking for her now?

And what of our escape? How will we...

I stalled my frenzied questioning and reminded myself to live in the moment. It was doing my sanity no good.

"I don't know what to do," Orlando said faintly. "I don't know how I will ever find my sister."

I was spared racking my brain for how to reply to him when the crunching of gravel sounded up the road. We ducked down, keeping only our eyes above the window sill so that we could watch. A tank was trundling down the road from our left. It moved quickly, passing directly beneath us. It continued on its course until it reached the crematorium's gates, where it ground to a halt. The barbed gate swung open automatically, and I expected the vehicle to trundle inside to park up along with the others in the parking lot. But it didn't. It moved forward only slightly, until it was half inside the gates, half out of them. And then, with the shuddering of metal, the entrance to the crematorium swung open. Out stepped ten armored IBSI members. They hurried toward the tank. Two hatches opened up on either side of it. The men surrounded the vehicle, reaching in through the openings and pulling out bodies. Dressed in the same patchwork clothing that many of the inmates of Bloodless Chicago wore, they had sacks strapped over their heads, and their wrists and ankles were bound together. *Corpses,* my brain immediately assumed, based on everything Orlando had told me of the tanks' purpose.

But my eyes told me something different.

The corpses were moving. Their limbs were struggling.

They were *alive.*

And yet the hunters began half-carrying, half-dragging them, one by one, from the tank, across the parking lot, and through the crematorium's steely entrance doors.

Orlando and I gaped, dumbstruck.

"Maura could be one of them!" he hissed. "She could have *been* one of them!"

The latter suggestion didn't sit right with me at all. I had seen each of the bodies they had pulled out, and none of them had been short enough to be Maura. Though I supposed that they could still have her in the tank. But again, that didn't make sense. The tank had come from the opposite direction from where Maura had been carried by the mutant.

But, apparently by desperation alone, Orlando was convinced.

"I need to go down and speak to them! Beg them, offer them anything!" His voice trailed off as he scurried to snatch up his wheel and remote, before dashing to the staircase of the building.

No, no, no.

I had a bad feeling about this. A very bad feeling. Not just for myself, but for Orlando, too.

Even if they were open to a barter, you didn't just bargain with the IBSI.

They bargained with you.

Chapter 21: Grace

I could only assume that Orlando had leapt down the flights of stairs in his manic hurry, for by the time I raced after him, he had already dashed out of the restaurant and emerged out in the street.

Crap.

I stalled, my heart hammering against my chest. I dared not call out to him as he ran. We were far too close to the hunters now. They were just on the other side of the building. Just a few dozen feet separated me from them.

Do I follow him? That would lead me, literally, into the IBSI's clutches.

I wasn't sure what exactly Orlando had meant by "offering them anything". One way or another, he had avoided handing me over to the IBSI until now, even though he could have easily done so. But now that he had lost his sister, I found it hard to believe that he wouldn't finally give in to the temptation.

As much as we had survived together in the past—how many hours or days had it been? I had totally lost track—blood ran thicker than water.

I decided to take a left turn and head in the opposite direction. I wanted to see if I could creep around the edge of the building and peer out on the other side while nobody was looking my way. At least then I could observe what was happening, what the heck Orlando's game plan was—not that I thought he had any semblance of a game plan. If I heard him begin to inform them about me, I would have to dash away like a madwoman... somewhere, anywhere.

I crept around the edge of the block, slowly and cautiously, trying not to cause the slightest crunch beneath my feet. All the while I held a lighter at the ready. I arrived at the end of the building and peered around to see that Orlando had already arrived in front of the tank—which the hunters were still unloading.

"Hey," he called. He looked so breathless and hurt as he staggered toward them, it was painful to watch. Even though he could be seconds away from ratting me out, my heart could not help but break for the sorry state of him.

"I think you have my sister," he gasped. "She's short, and looks very similar to me. She was abducted by one of your beasts. Please. I *need* her. If you could—"

Orlando's pleas were cut short as one of the hunters sprang out of the tank. He moved up to Orlando with supernatural speed and, without warning, withdrew a needle from his pocket and stabbed it into Orlando's neck. Orlando's eyes bulged. The blade-wheel and remote slipped from his grasp. He dropped to the ground like a fly.

It all happened so abruptly, I let out an involuntary gasp. A gasp that immediately became my downfall. I had lost my helmet during my escape from the gang of criminals, and now I had nothing to hide behind. Their attention shot in my direction before I could back away behind the building. Recognition flashed in their eyes instantly.

Before any of the hunters could lurch for me, I blazed

up a shield of fire. Every instinct screamed at me to dart in the opposite direction—run for my life while I still could. But... Orlando. I could still just about make him out through my fire, lying there on the ground. What were they going to do to him? Carry him into the crematorium along with those other hapless souls and burn him alive?

What the hell were these people thinking?

My hesitation soon left me out of options. My shield of fire was so thick in parts that I could hardly see through it. I hadn't noticed three hunters circle and creep up behind me.

I heard what could have only been the clicking of guns. "Relinquish the flames! You have ten seconds."

My breathing ragged, I reminded myself that they would not kill me. Not yet... or would they?

One of them fired a bullet in the air, painfully close. My eardrums reverberated from the sound.

More hunters hurried to make a wide circle and joined those who'd gathered behind me.

Two hunters picked up Orlando from the ground, placed a sack over his head, and then began to carry him through the gate, along with several other hunters carrying what appeared to be the last of the bodies from the tank.

I surged forward into the road that bordered one side of the crematorium compound, adjacent from the one I'd been standing on, in an attempt to distance myself from the men behind me. But here more hunters closed in on me from my right and my left, blocking both sides of the road.

It seemed that I would have no option but to just rush toward one of the encroaching groups. It would mean risking them shooting at me, and banking on them leaping aside at the last moment to avoid being burned.

But then a horde of mutants descended.

Their arrival was announced by bloodcurdling screeches overhead. Their beady eyes were set on me as their heavy wings beat, their beaks and talons clacking while they touched down with heavy thumps on the wet road.

I knew from experience that these beasts were far less afraid of fire. They weren't immune to it, but they were much more daring in the face of it. They gained even more confidence when in a group.

Looking frantically toward the two men carrying Orlando across the parking lot and toward the entrance of the crematorium, I realized that now, ironically, inside the compound was the only direction that was not cornered off by mutants and hunters. *Into the crematorium.*

It felt like my brain had shut down as I darted forward, all the while maintaining my blaze. But as I reached the tank parked half inside, half outside the gate, an idea flashed through my brain. I verified in the space of a second that its open interior was emptied of victims before exuding into it the most intense billows of fire that I could manage. Then I stooped, shooting flames toward the tank's underbelly, near where I hoped the fuel tank was. It caught fire shockingly fast. I backed away into the compound, bracing myself for the explosion.

I had no choice now but to move into the jaws of death—the crematorium's compound. But I hoped that the tank would explode, forcing the hunters and mutants to scramble, and provide me with the option to back out again and…

And then it happened. The explosion came sooner than I had dared hope for. Almost too soon; I had barely gotten myself out of the way. I had doused the tank with my fire so fiercely that barely a few seconds later it went off like a bomb. The force of the blast shot outward, causing me to stumble and fall to the ground.

I heard the shouts of men and squealing of mutants,

even as I fought to stand up again.

I gazed toward the metal entrance of the crematorium just in time to witness the doors slam shut. *No! Dammit!*

More screeching sounded, much closer this time, and less desperate than a few seconds ago. The mutants had recovered more quickly from the shock of the blast than the hunters. I glimpsed them flying over the wall toward me and my blazing aura.

My eyes traveled wildly around the parking lot until my focus fixed on the large number of tanks stored in here. I raced up to the nearest one and doused it with fire, just as I had done the first, and then raced onward until I set up a chain of explosions, one tank after the other.

As they went off in a symphony, I hurled myself toward a narrow passageway that wound round the back of the building, in between the fence and the crematorium's back wall, in order to avoid the brunt of the explosions.

I raced down the narrow path while gazing up hopelessly at the crematorium's towering brick wall on my right. Even though I had spotted no windows when inspecting it from a distance, I was half hoping that I would see one now—lower down in the building—that I could break into, just to get away from the mutants whom

I knew would be following me anytime now. The explosions that I'd set off were nothing but distractions to delay their chase.

But there were no windows. And as I reached the end of passageway, I realized I'd hit a dead end. I'd assumed that it would extend all the way around the building. *Dammit, wasn't that a logical assumption?* It didn't matter whether it was logical or not. As I whirled around to face the direction I'd just run from, behind me and on either side of me was impenetrable brick wall. And now, in front of me, was the harrowing sight of the first of the mutants galloping toward me, their wingspan being too broad for the narrow passage.

Somehow, watching them lope was far more terrifying than watching them fly. Gone was any grace they might have had in flight. They looked ten times more menacing, less birdlike and more beastlike.

"No!" I roared. "No!"

I'm not going to be brought back into the IBSI's clutches. I'm not.

I manipulated my fire to spread as far in front of me as I possibly could, and managed to stall them in their gallop about ten feet away from me. But how long would they stay at this distance? How long would it be before the first of them braved the flames, plunged into the heat and grabbed me? Or maybe they would do no such thing. Maybe they would just stand there, ensuring that I was trapped with nowhere to run, and wait for their masters to arrive with sedative arrows. Arrows that would penetrate the flames and shoot right into my...

"Grace!" a voice boomed down from above me. A voice that was so familiar, I would have recognized it underwater.

Relief rolled through every fiber of my being, hot tears brimming in my eyes.

"Dad!" I cried.

Through my flames, I made out three figures flying over the crowd of mutants and descending on me. My dad was at the lead, followed closely by my great-uncle Lucas, and Kailyn. All three were in their solid state. My father's face shone with sweat, his green eyes wide and alert and gleaming in the firelight.

"Dad!" I gasped again. The word felt like honey on my tongue.

He swooped down toward me, and the next thing I knew, his strong arms had wrapped around me and I was being lifted upward.

My trembling form blanketed around him. I buried my head against his chest and locked my arms around his neck so tightly I was probably strangling him.

Oh, my God, Dad!

"You found me," I panted. "You found me!"

It felt like every single emotion I'd experienced in the past few days bubbled to the surface at once. All the stress, the fear, the uncertainty. I could no longer hold back my tears.

"It's okay, baby," he breathed, even as he heaved a deep sigh of relief. "You're safe now. I've got you."

I dared glance down beneath us and was surprised to see the mutants hadn't followed us. Then I realized why. Kailyn and Lucas had distracted them. They had created a billowing ceiling of flames over the mutants, blinding them completely from looking up toward us, and likely burning them to a crisp if they didn't escape back down the passageway fast enough. I figured the combined power of two full fae blasting down on them at once would be enough to seriously injure them.

My father kept flying higher with me, his grip only tightening around my waist, until we had flown so high into the night sky that the mutants' screeching became distant. A cool wind whipped against us. I gazed behind us, toward the lake. The beautiful, seemingly endless lake. The lake that had been so utterly unattainable to us.

"I'm sorry, Dad," I rasped. "I'm so sorry." Now that I'd reunited with him, all the guilt for having left and gotten myself into such a mess resurfaced. It tore me apart to imagine how worried sick I must've made him and my mother.

"We need to get you back home," he said, planting a firm kiss against my forehead.

I wanted to ask how he'd managed to find me in the first place, but something much more urgent was tugging at me. My eyes returned to the crematorium beneath us. *Orlando. He's still down there. Maybe even Maura too, if she got taken inside.*

"Dad," I broached, nodding down toward the large building, "I have at least one friend trapped in there."

"Friend?" he asked, moving his head backward so that he could look me in the eye. He was frowning.

Well, "friend" might've been too strong a word, especially since I had no idea whether Orlando might've been on the verge of ratting me out to the hunters before one stabbed him with a syringe. And Maura had been more than willing to hand me over to the IBSI at the first opportunity. Still, in this city of nightmares and desolation, without those two, I highly doubted that I would still be alive. Heck, I never would've made it out of that sewage tunnel that the Bloodless had chased me down soon after I'd woken up here.

And they had saved me from a lot of crap since then, too.

"They're siblings," I replied. "A brother and a sister. I wouldn't be here with you now if it weren't for them. They helped me survive. I know for a fact that the brother, Orlando, was taken down there, I saw it with my own eyes. And I think the sister, Maura, might be there too."

"Down in *that*?" my father asked, still confused. "What is that, exactly?"

"A crematorium," I replied, though that hardly served to clear his confusion. I was still confused myself as to why they were dragging living people into it. "Orlando and Maura said that's what it is. But th-they're taking people in there alive. I don't know what they're doing with them, but what else would they do to them in a crematorium other than…"

My father exhaled as my voice trailed off. "So you'd like me to go look for your friends?"

No, I really didn't want that. I didn't want my father to let go of me now that he had found me. But I owed it to those siblings. Besides, as a fae, it shouldn't be too difficult a task for my father to pull off. He could thin himself at will and go undetected by the IBSI... Hopefully he wouldn't be too late.

"I would," I said, my voice strained.

"What do they look like?" he asked.

I described them to him as best as I could. Maura was short, but for all I knew there could be lots of other short young women down there, too. God knew how many people they'd hoarded. The fact that all inmates on this side of the city had shaven heads made my father's task more difficult; it caused them all to look more indistinguishable. More uniform. Orlando was easier to describe than his sister because of his injured shoulder.

"Okay," my father said, his voice deep. "Once Kailyn and Lucas get back up here, one of them will take you back to The Shade. I think Kailyn should do that, and I'll ask Lucas to accompany me down into the crematorium."

"Thank you," I said, even as I felt another twinge of

guilt. After all the trouble I'd caused, it felt like the last thing I ought to be doing was causing more potential trouble for my father.

We didn't have to wait long for Lucas and Kailyn to return. They finished chasing off the mutants quickly and hurtled back up toward us.

"Hello," Lucas said, eyeing me. He reached out a hand and mussed my already thoroughly mussed and matted hair. "You look like you've been having fun."

I coughed out a dry half-laugh. "Yeah," I managed weakly.

"Lucas," my father said, turning to my great-uncle, "I'm not finished here yet. I need to go down to search that large building—a crematorium. There are two young people I need to look for. Will you come with me?"

He shrugged. "Yeah, all right. Which two young people?"

"More on that in a minute," my father replied. He faced Kailyn and addressed her. "I need you to return Grace to The Shade right now. God knows what injuries she's sustained while she's been here. Take her to the hospital and have her seen immediately."

"Right," Kailyn said, her jaw setting. My father

transferred me to Kailyn's open arms, and I clung on to her like a monkey.

I cast one last glance at my father.

"Thank you, Dad," I said. "And please, be careful."

He nodded, offering me a small smile, before turning to Lucas to continue conversing with him.

Then Kailyn drew us away from the two and began hurtling away with me, back toward the heart of the city. She traveled with such speed that I struggled to keep my eyes open. Which wasn't a bad thing. I closed my eyes on the dead city and all its horrors slipping away beneath us, and nestled my forehead against the crook of Kailyn's neck.

Home.

I'm going home.

CHAPTER 22: BEN

After witnessing Atticus' conversation in his office, we discovered the river running right by the IBSI's compound. From there, we began soaring over the ruined city, scouring the roads for signs of the hunters' presence. The hunters were like bloodhounds. I figured that it wouldn't take them long to locate Grace, and heading in the direction they were heading seemed like the best strategy.

The majority of hunter activity had appeared to be along the coast. We traveled there and continued searching until explosions caught our attention further up the shore, and we were pulled in that direction immediately. Then I heard Grace yelling. And I found my baby girl.

Truth be told, I didn't need a lot of convincing from my daughter to venture down to the crematorium. Ever since I'd glimpsed Atticus' laptop screen, those eight words had been etched at the back of my mind.

"Fight for Open Education on the Bloodless Antidote."

What, exactly, did that mean? Now that we had found Grace, she was safe with Kailyn, and I knew that she would soon reach The Shade, my mind had room to mull over this question thoroughly.

Besides, we had come all this way, and now that I was here, I wanted to sniff around a bit more and try to piece together some clues.

Lucas and I thinned ourselves and then descended on the giant crematorium. Passing the smoking chimneys, we needed to decide from which direction to first enter the building. Lucas figured that the front was as good as any place to start, and so we dipped down to the parking lot, which was still blazing. We moved through the heavy metal entrance—above which was fixed an old, rickety sign, "Lakeside Crematorium"—and emerged in the interior of the building.

The entrance chamber was an oblong, stark white room lit by fluorescent ceiling strips. It contained not a single piece of furniture; its only purpose seemed to be to lead to the next room, which was guarded by a steel door that looked as sturdy as the main entrance.

Passing through this one and arriving on the other side, Lucas and I stopped short. We gaped.

This... this wasn't a crematorium. Perhaps the building had once been used as such, but now... it was some kind of colossal, multi-layered laboratory. It was built like an atrium, with a concave ceiling that extended high overhead. Including the ground floor that sprawled out in front of us, I counted ten levels altogether. Countless hunters dressed in black uniforms milled about the aisles, and each level was jam-packed with rows of stainless-steel tables and filled with chemistry apparatus—except the top two floors. Those platforms appeared to consist of... cages. At least, based on what we could see of them from here.

Lucas and I moved upward and landed on the ninth level. We found ourselves gazing around at a maze of cages filled with Bloodless. I had no idea what the cages were made of, but they must have been strong to withstand the way many of them were ripping at the bars.

There were only a few hunters we could spot up here, moving among the rows of cells.

"I wonder why on earth they're keeping them caged up in here," Lucas muttered beneath his breath. "There are more than enough of these things outside."

We continued scoping out the floor until we came full circle on ourselves. We barely spotted a single one of the hundreds of cages that did not contain a Bloodless.

"Let's check the floor above us," I whispered.

We floated upward, landing on yet another level filled with cages. But these were not filled with Bloodless. These were occupied by pale, sickly-looking people. My immediate instinct was to label them as half-bloods, but I wasn't so sure. Somehow, they looked more ill than the conventional half-blood—like River used to look.

Although their heads were mostly shaven, their hair was very thin, with barely enough body to cover the white of their scalps. Their skin was so thin it showed an unhealthy number of veins. And they were very, very pale.

What are these hunters playing at?

"Look over there... the back of this row," Lucas whispered.

Having been looking down the row to our left, I turned

and looked to our right, and saw it. About twenty of the same type of pale humans, all lined up in a row next to each other. They sat upright, their backs against the wall. Surrounding them was a scattering of brown fabric bags and a trio of hunters. The reason for the hostages' rigidness became clear. The hunters were armed and were aiming their guns threateningly at them.

Lucas and I froze and watched as one of the IBSI members stooped down and grabbed the arm of one of the men—a middle-aged man with a harsh, triangular jaw and scars marring almost every inch of his face.

"You'll be coming with me," the hunter said in a low voice.

He pulled the man up and stood him against one of the cages. Then he returned to the cluster and picked out another person—a woman this time, perhaps in her late twenties. I reminded myself of the reason I was down here in the first place—to reclaim Grace's friends—and became immediately alert to verify that the woman was not Maura. It seemed that she wasn't. This woman was tall, I estimated about five foot ten. Besides, she had light hair, not dark like Maura was supposed to have.

The hunter then stooped for a third person—another

middle-aged man. Once he had them all lined up in a row, he nudged their backs, indicating that they move forward… toward us.

Even though we had thinned ourselves, we backed up anyway and let them pass. The hunters remaining withdrew syringes from a bag hanging on the outside of one of the cages before they began forcibly sedating each one of the crowd. The drug was practically instantaneous. Only seconds after the needle had sunk through their flesh, their heads lolled and they slid into a lying position on the floor.

We waited for the two hunters to leave the group of unconscious people before approaching. I examined each of them carefully. Then, right at the back of the group, I spotted a young man with a bloody, injured shoulder. There was a large man in front of him who must've been blocking my view of him before now.

This youth fit the description. He had to be Orlando.

I quickly looked around us to verify that there were no more hunters nearby. On spotting none, I addressed my uncle. "Okay, this is one of them. Now let's search the rest of this level to see if we can find his sister."

I double-checked that I hadn't missed Maura among

this cluster of bodies, and on seeing that I hadn't, we began moving strategically along the rows of cells in search of the girl. We didn't spot her in any of them. We came across a few shortish women, but none of them looked even remotely similar to Orlando.

If Maura wasn't up here, among the other people of her kind, I couldn't think where she would be. Perhaps she hadn't been brought to this so-called crematorium after all and Grace had been mistaken.

We headed back to Orlando.

"So it looks like we're going to have to forget about the girl," I whispered to Lucas. "She doesn't seem to be in here. At least we found this guy… Now we need to think about the best way to get him out."

"Well," Lucas replied, "we'll just make a run for it. Scoop him up and head to the exit—we'll be out before any of them realize what happened."

"Right," I agreed.

Lucas and I solidified ourselves and swiftly picked Orlando up. We dashed toward the edge of the floor, but just before we dove over the edge, bone-chilling screaming made us stop short in our tracks. It was the screaming of a man.

"What the..." Lucas breathed.

It sounded like it was coming from directly beneath us, an estimation that seemed to be confirmed when a second noise pierced through the atrium. Screeching. The screeching of Bloodless. *What is going on?*

I shifted Orlando's weight to Lucas. "Take Orlando and get out of here. I'm going to thin myself and check out what the heck is going on down there."

I was glad when Lucas didn't argue—I'd thought he might want to come with me too. Juggling Orlando's full weight, which frankly wasn't much due to his light build, Lucas bolted with Orlando over the floor's barrier and hurtled toward the exit. As Lucas had predicted, by the time the hunters had been alerted to his and Orlando's forms darting through the air, he had already reached the first exit. Satisfied that Lucas needed no help from me, I reassumed my subtle form and lowered myself to the level beneath—the Bloodless' level.

The hunters who'd left the upper level were standing outside one of the cages in a corner. I moved closer and witnessed the source of the scream and the screech. The scar-faced man had been locked inside the cage. He was crammed up against its wall on the floor while a Bloodless crawled over him and tore into his neck. I zoomed closer, barely even breathing as I gaped.

The man was already beginning to shake and tremble—the first signs of turning into one of those dreaded creatures. One of the hunters was gripping a long, extendable syringe. As the man's trembling intensified, the hunter dug the needle through the bars of the cage and caught his neck on the side that the Bloodless wasn't occupying. The hunter pulled a small lever at the side of the spearlike syringe and drew out what looked like a couple hundred milliliters' worth of blood. He pulled the syringe back through the bars and held it upright. After several minutes, the Bloodless voluntarily climbed off the man, who was now vibrating so violently his limbs lifted off the floor, like he was being jolted with volts of electricity. The Bloodless rose to its feet... and that was when it struck me how short it was.

I looked closer still, trying to make out the distinctive facial features this noseless monster had once had. It was incredibly difficult but... as my eyes lowered to its chest, I could make out an ever so slight bump of breasts. This indicated that the Bloodless was only newly turned, for after a while, Bloodless' fat deposits wasted away completely and they tended to look androgynous.

I stopped breathing for a moment as a chilling thought crept into my mind.

Could this Bloodless be Maura?

Having never seen her, and only having Grace's vague description to go by, there was no way I could say for certain. All I knew was that I hadn't been able to find the girl even though Grace had suspected that she had been brought down here, this Bloodless was the right height, and she was clearly newly turned.

But whether she was or was not Maura, there was nothing I could do now. She was gone either way.

I shuddered internally, witnessing the Bloodless extend her tongue to lick away the streams of blood spilling from either side of her mouth.

And I once again questioned myself:

What are these hunters doing?

CHAPTER 23: GRACE

I kept my eyes closed for most of the journey back to The Shade. I didn't want to open them again until we'd arrived, safe within the island.

Visions of that city still haunted me. Its darkness, its hopelessness. I could still practically feel its chill in my bones, even as we crossed the ocean toward warmer weather.

I kept thinking about Orlando and his sister. If they were still alive, I was sure that my father and great-uncle would find them. And then they would come back to The Shade, and I would have finally fulfilled my promise to them… even if they had failed to help me reach a phone in the end.

"Well, looks like we're here," Kailyn said cheerfully, causing my eyelids to shoot open. Gazing at the waves churning beneath us, I caught sight of the familiar rock formation outside The Shade's boundary. We were nearing the island's port.

Kailyn hovered with me over the invisible barrier and we moved closer to where she estimated the mainland was. Then we began yelling down for somebody to let us in. It was Corrine who emerged, Arwen following close behind her. I had never seen either of them look so relieved as they rushed toward us in the air.

Corrine wrapped her arms around me as I clung to Kailyn and pressed a deep kiss against my cheek.

"Thank God you're all right, Grace. You wouldn't believe the earful I've given Arwen for taking you to Hawaii. I mean, dammit, Grace, what were you thinking? You went venturing out to practically the exact spot where your father and aunt first got into trouble—"

I was spared from answering Corrine as Arwen rushed forward and hugged me tight.

"How are you?" she asked, her face stricken with guilt.

"I'm so sorry."

"It's not your fault!" I exclaimed. Then I addressed Corrine. "It really wasn't Arwen's fault. She took me to Hawaii only because I requested it. She was doing me a huge favor."

Before Corrine could respond, Kailyn said, "Ben said we need to take Grace to the hospital right away and check her out."

My mind turned back to the wound in my leg, where the Bloodless had bitten me. It still tingled slightly, though it had stopped stinging. I hadn't had the chance to look at it for ages. There had been far too many things going on and my injury had become the last thing on my mind.

Corrine performed her routine identity check, then allowed Kailyn and me through the barrier. Together we headed directly to the hospital. They took me to one of the long-stay rooms, equipped with a television which was playing some news channel in the background and even a small shelf of books. But the only thing I was interested in at this moment was the soft, warm bed. When they laid me down on it, I turned to Kailyn, about to request that she go inform my mother and the rest of my family that I was back, but the fae had already anticipated my request.

"I'll fetch your mom and everyone else now."

She hurried off, leaving me with Arwen and Corrine.

"So," Corrine began, standing at my bedside. "I won't ask you to recount everything now, since you'll only have to repeat it again when your mother arrives. You must tell me, however, any injuries you might have sustained, and how you're feeling in general."

I considered the latter question first. *How am I feeling?* It felt like a part of me was still shellshocked, to be honest. The last twenty-four hours especially had just been a blur of one insane, terrifying situation after the other.

I blew out a breath, and leaned back against my pillows. "I'm feeling... relieved. That's all I'm feeling right now," I replied.

"And are there no injuries you need me to look at? Nothing at all?" She raised her eyebrows, surprised.

I showed her the finger I suspected was broken, and she healed it within a matter of minutes. Then I cleared my throat, and reached down to tug at my pants. "This leg," I said, raising it tentatively. "You should take a look at this leg." Even as I said the words, I was bracing myself for the witch's reaction.

I'd predicted it precisely. Her mouth dropped open as

she glimpsed the fang wounds. Her eyes shot to me, wide with horror.

"Grace," she gasped. "What… You were *bitten?*"

I swallowed hard, and nodded.

"By a Bloodless?" Arwen asked, looking just as petrified as her mother.

I nodded again. "But I haven't turned yet… obviously. And this happened like, over twenty-four hours ago now, I think. I think my being half fae has counteracted it. I-I'm still okay."

Corrine fell silent. She and Arwen leaned over closer to my wounds to inspect them. Then Corrine looked me over from head to toe.

She straightened. "Right," she said, letting out a breath. "We're going to have to hope you'll be fine, since as you well know, neither the witches nor the jinn of The Shade are able to counteract the venom." A tense silence followed her words. "You… you haven't experienced any symptoms at all?" she asked, almost disbelieving.

"No," I replied quickly. "I mean, the wounds stung like hell at first, and they still tingle a bit, but they're deep wounds that still haven't fully healed over…"

"No trembling, shivering, etc?" she pressed.

I was about to blurt out, "No," again, but it wasn't exactly true that I hadn't been shivering. I had felt cold a lot while I'd been in Chicago, but anyone would have. I'd been drenched to the bone in rainwater much of the time, for heaven's sake. I realized that I did still feel rather cold even now, but my clothes were still damp, and this room was pretty chilly. "No," I replied firmly. "Nothing."

"Okay," Corrine said. "Well, I'm going to examine you further, but the first thing you should do is take a shower and clean yourself up."

"Agreed," I said. I couldn't nod vigorously enough.

The witches stripped me out of my filthy clothes and ushered me into the bathroom. Here I ran the shower, as hot as it would go, and stepped inside. I cherished the clean, steaming water like it was liquid gold as it beat down against my back. I rinsed all the muck off my body and washed my hair thoroughly, applying four rounds of conditioner just to get it free from tangles. The rash that had broken out on my skin from the contaminated river water had faded now.

By the time I stepped out of the bathroom, wearing a pair of fresh cotton pajamas I'd found in one of the closets, my heart leapt to see that my mother and family were already waiting for me in the bedroom.

My mother's face lit up like fireworks. I leapt into her arms and held her tight, even as she kissed my cheeks over and over again. "Oh, Grace! You have *no idea* how worried I've been!"

"I know, Mom. And I'm sorry."

My mom wouldn't let me go for another five minutes. She held onto me like a mother bear. When I finally backed away, I moved to greet my grandmother, Sofia, who was next in line, then my grandfather, Derek, my other grandmother, Nadia, my aunts Rose, Lalia and Dafne, Uncle Caleb and Jamil, great-grandfather Aiden, great-aunt and uncle Vivienne and Xavier, and finally Victoria, Hazel and Benedict, who'd also come along to see me. Kailyn had returned, too.

I hugged the rest of my family one by one, curious to know what had been going on with everyone while I'd been away. Benedict was the last to embrace me. As I pulled away, he said with a grin, "I sure have missed you, Gracie…"

Taking in Benedict's boyish face, I realized that I truly meant it when I replied, "And I missed you too, squirt." Before my cousin could tack on a misplaced comment which I sensed was seconds from rolling off his tongue, I turned to my mother. "I've got a lot to tell you guys," I said.

Corrine brought in some extra chairs for everyone to take a seat around my bed, while I sank into the mattress and leaned against the headboard.

"I want to see your wounds before anything else, Grace," my mother said, anxiety washing over her relief. A part of me had been kind of hoping Corrine wouldn't have mentioned them to my family yet. I'd wanted to give them at least a short breather from worrying about me. But of course Corrine would have clued them in.

My mother rolled up my pants to reveal my cleaned bite marks. Her breath hitched. Everyone crowded over my bed and stared down at them.

"You've really experienced no symptoms?" my mother asked.

"No," I replied, feeling more confident in my answer this time. I felt warmer now after my hot shower. Perhaps Corrine had turned up the heat in this room, too. I instinctively clutched my blankets around me all the same, finding them comforting.

"I had wanted to do a full examination on her before

you arrived," Corrine explained to my mother, "but I suppose it was stupid of me to think I could fit it in before you guys came rushing in. And now you are here, I guess I have to wait until she's finished telling her story... though I would much prefer to check her out now."

"I don't have any other injuries," I told the witch confidently. I'd been bashed about a lot—I had bruises and cuts aplenty, for sure—but I hadn't noticed anything else very serious in the shower. "I'm okay," I said, offering them a smile. "Really, the examination can wait. Now, I'd like to tell you everything."

"First tell us where your father is," my mother requested, nervous.

"He and Lucas should be arriving anytime now," I explained. "They stayed back because, well, I made a couple of friends while I was in Chicago, and they were in trouble—I asked him to help them. Dad and Lucas are probably on their way back now, as we speak. Maybe even nearing the island. It's been a while since we left them."

"Okay," my mother said, loosening up a little. She reached out and held my hand. "So start at the beginning."

And so I did. I took my mind back to everything that had happened since my parents departed with the League for the ogres' kingdom.

I told them about my investigation into Georgina's background, my visit to her parents in the UK, how Arwen and I ended up in Hawaii, and then my eventual capture and escape into Bloodless territory. My father returned at this point in the story. He and Lucas hurried into the room, and to my delight, they were carrying Orlando.

I leapt off the bed and hurried to them.

"Is he okay?" I whispered, checking his pulse.

"Well, as you can see, he's breathing," my father replied.

"Hardly looks okay though, does he?" Lucas muttered.

As okay as a terminally ill person can be...

My gaze rose to my father. "And Maura?" I asked hopefully, even though I had already assumed they had not been able to find her.

My father shook his head darkly.

Ouch. I couldn't say that I would exactly miss the girl, but that would be a tough pill for Orlando to swallow when he woke up.

"Arwen," Corrine said, "take this lad into one of the spare rooms and have someone look at him."

Arwen obeyed her mother, approaching Orlando and vanishing the two of them from the spot.

I rose to my feet. My mother was already wrapped in my father's arms, greeting him. I hugged Lucas in the meantime, thanking him, and then gave my father a proper greeting when my mother had stepped back.

Then I returned to my bed, Lucas and my father taking seats around me with the others.

Although I still hadn't finished my story, and indeed, I would have to start again for my father and Lucas, I was too anxious to hear what my father had seen in the crematorium and where exactly he had found Orlando. I fired the questions at him in quick succession.

My father's brow was furrowed, and I noticed for the first time how... distant he looked. Although he sat just feet away from me, his mind still seemed far away. He cleared his throat.

"Something very odd is going on with the IBSI," he said finally. His voice was surprisingly hoarse. He locked eyes with my grandfather Derek, who raised his brows in question.

"What?" my grandfather asked.

My father stood and began pacing up and down by my bed. Then his gaze returned to me. "Grace, that *crematorium* was not a crematorium."

"Huh?" I asked, wrinkling my nose in confusion.

"It was not a crematorium," he repeated. "It was a massive laboratory, with whole floors containing cages of Bloodless and people like Orlando. They are using the Bloodless for something. We witnessed them feeding one of the sickly humans—a man—to a Bloodless in a cage who, uh, I have a suspicion was actually Maura."

My jaw dropped. "W-What? Are you serious?"

"Of course I could be mistaken, but she was the right height..." He let his words linger in the air for several moments before continuing, "As they fed the man to the Bloodless, they withdrew blood from him as he was in the process of turning. They're doing *some kind* of major experimentation, or major research... or... I don't know what." He exhaled in frustration, his expression growing more agitated.

"Ben," my grandfather said, "you need to start from the beginning for the rest of us. We have no idea what you're talking about."

"Yes, yes, I know," my father said, still disconnected. He took a seat again and recounted the first part of his story that I also had not heard—how he'd left The Shade and managed to figure out that I was in Chicago.

"We scoured the Chicago HQ," Ben explained, "and we managed to locate Atticus's room. He was on the phone to someone, and he referred to Grace having leapt into the river before escaping into the other part of the city." He stopped abruptly, his disturbed expression returning. "Dammit, they're up to something. I caught sight of something on his computer screen. *Fight for open education on the Bloodless antidote.* But he slammed the laptop shut before I could read further, and then I needed to…"

I barely heard the rest of my father's sentence. I almost choked on my tongue as the words trickled through my brain.

Fight for open education on the Bloodless antidote.

F for Fight… O for Open… E for…

"*Oh, my God!*" I practically screamed, leaping from my bed like a Jack-in-the-Box and scaring the crap out of everyone. "FOEBA!" I stammered. "That's what damn FOEBA must stand for! Fight for Open Education on the Bloodless Antidote!"

A silence descended on the room. Everyone stared at me.

My father's eyes widened. "So it does…" he breathed.

A dozen questions flooded my mind. Did a Bloodless

antidote really exist? Was it Georgina who had discovered it? Why was she having to fight to educate people about it? For heaven's sake, millions of the IBSI's resources were invested every year just in keeping the Bloodless away from human settlements. If there was a cure, they should be the first to leap on it.

Why would the IBSI want to keep it such a secret?

"Antidote," my grandfather Derek repeated, a profound expression on his face. "I wonder what that could be?"

Everyone looked at each other blankly.

"Whatever it is," I said, "the IBSI are hell-bent on stifling information about it. And Georgina... Lawrence's mother. Somehow she discovered it... and she was on the run somewhere."

"Before she got conveniently killed in an accident," Shayla finished. I looked up to see the witch standing in the doorway of the hospital room. I hadn't even noticed her arrive.

"Yes," I breathed.

I just knew that she had been fleeing from Atticus. But would he really have killed his own wife? I supposed it would've been easy enough for him to have her assassinated and then make the whole thing look like an accident.

And what of Lawrence? What exactly did Atticus have planned for him?

"Well, I just witnessed firsthand that the IBSI have uses for the Bloodless," my father said. "Whatever the exact uses are, it seems clear that they want to keep the Bloodless alive and thriving."

That would certainly explain why Atticus did not want copies of Georgina's files lying about, even if they were encrypted. Some non-IBSI tech-savvy geek might have been able to crack them.

And did those files really contain information, like, actual details about the cure? There had certainly been enough files on that thumb drive.

So, Georgina. I continued to mull it over. It seemed like she had started—or been trying to start—some kind of underground movement to try to spread this knowledge. Wherever she had planned to go with Lawrence after she left Atticus, it must have been somewhere she thought was safe, where she believed she could further her mission... or maybe it had been solely out of fear of her husband.

Another thing was clear at least: Whoever Georgina had been, she obviously couldn't have agreed with her husband's way of doing things. And then somehow he must have found out about her activities or intentions…

I clutched my blanket closer, feeling unnerved.

How deep do these lies go? For all I knew, we might have still only touched the very tip of the iceberg of the IBSI's deception.

"Oh, my. Th-That's Lawrence!" my mother exclaimed suddenly beside me. "On national news!"

She was staring at the television screen, playing noiselessly in the background.

My eyes bulged.

Filling the frame of the news channel was a young man who looked unmistakably like Lawrence Conway. He was… *standing.* Standing on a platform in some kind of small, bare, stark white room, wearing just a pair of boxer shorts. He no longer looked pale or sickly. His handsome face, stoic and still shaven like the last time I'd seen him, had a healthy complexion to it, almost a glow. And his dusty blond hair, which had been trimmed shorter, looked thicker, healthier.

The platform he was standing on swiveled, showcasing his body like he was some kind of specimen… which, I realized, he was.

He was tall, just like I'd suspected he would be if he'd been able to stand upright. And his build was bulkier, his muscles toned—also as I had believed they must've been.

I jolted from the bed so hard that I tripped on my own feet and smacked my knee against one of the low bedside tables.

"Grace!" several voices admonished me at once in concern, but I lifted myself up before they could do anything and staggered forward to the mantelpiece, which held the remote. I grabbed it and turned up the volume.

"… momentous milestone for the IBSI," the voiceover of a female newscaster was announcing. "The drug is yet to be named and it is still being trialed, but we have been lucky enough to gain a first glimpse of the results."

I moved up closer to the screen, where I could take in Lawrence in more detail. As the platform swiveled round so that he was facing the camera directly, I gazed into his tawny brown eyes. Brown eyes that seemed faded, distant. As though he was not quite present.

I suddenly felt a twinge in my chest. A deep, throbbing ache. I was taken aback by how strong it was.

Lawrence.

What have they done to you?

"The test subject," the newscaster went on, "whose name has been withheld for privacy reasons, successfully completed the procedure. According to our IBSI correspondent, the young man has developed combat abilities that have surprised even the organization itself. We were not able to procure exact details but no doubt they will be disclosed in the coming months, as more trials are carried out. On questioning, the IBSI confirmed that there is currently no estimate when—or if—the drug will be available to the public, but discussions are certainly underway. We hope that we will be able to provide demonstrations of the test subject's abilities in the coming weeks at the IBSI's discretion. But for now, this breakthrough serves to demonstrate IBSI's continued commitment to protecting our borders, and reducing the loss of lives of the courageous young men and women who fight to keep us safe at night."

Lawrence disappeared from the screen. It felt like somebody had just switched off a light. Hollowness pooled in the pit of my stomach.

What are you now, Lawrence?

I was still reeling from the shock of seeing him again. The last time I'd laid eyes on him, he'd been a frail, fragile thing, incapable of even supporting his own weight. Now, here he was, the absolute polar opposite. Exuding strength and prowess, he stood tall and, frankly, downright intimidating. I'd always known that he had the build of a fighter, but whatever procedure he had recently undergone had taken him to levels even my imagination had never reached.

As much as it relieved me to see that he was still alive, and that not only had he regained use of his limbs, he was healthy and possessing such newfound strength, his expression had just seemed so... far away. Lost. He looked like a totally different person.

As the news switched to covering a merfolk incident off the coast of Florida, we gazed at each other, stunned.

"What did they do to him exactly?" my mother said quietly.

My legs felt weak. I staggered backward. The backs of my legs touching the bed frame, I dropped down on the mattress among my blankets.

"God knows—" I began to murmur... then I choked.

My speech was cut short by a sudden tremor running through my body. It felt like it erupted from within the very core of me and sent vibrations throughout my limbs.

Losing control, I found myself slamming backward on the mattress and shaking like I was undergoing some kind of fit.

I was barely aware of the faces crowding around me, the hands trying to steady me. All I could do was lie there as tremors rolled through me in waves.

And then I experienced another sensation: coldness. Deep in the marrow of my bones. As iciness consumed me, rendering me practically breathless, a truth was forced to the forefront of my mind that I'd fought to push back ever since my encounter with the Bloodless in the sewage tunnel.

I'd felt cold non-stop since then.

Though I'd had plenty of excuses to feel cold—the weather, the lack of sufficient clothing, the conditions I'd been traveling in—the truth remained: I'd been cold. And even now, although I'd convinced myself I felt warmer after my shower, the reality was I'd been clutching at blankets ever since entering this room.

I realized why I'd been averse to Corrine's in-depth examination of me. My subconscious had feared what she might find.

Two hands moved to my forehead now. My mother's

and father's.

Then the tremors relinquished as suddenly as they had started. But the coldness remained.

Winded, I sat bolt upright, gazing around the room in a panic. My family's voices were a blur as doubt and fear paralyzed my brain.

Maybe I was turning into a Bloodless after all.

Maybe Maura was right: half of me was still human. The process was just delayed because of my fae blood.

Delayed but not counteracted.

Oh, God…

How much time do I have left?

Chapter 24: Bastien

My journey to visit the chieftains of the packs who lived nearest to our lair went more smoothly than I could have hoped for. Although their behavior was often perfunctory, each of them welcomed me and my Blackhall companions into their homes, and were more than agreeable to sit and talk. We discussed how we might form strategic alliances and help each other in the future, should there ever be a need to defend ourselves again from outside threats. I extended our resources for their use, should they ever need them, and they did the same for us.

The journey soon became almost... tiresome. It felt all too easy. And I had been hoping that traveling would take my mind off Victoria, but if anything, it only made me think of her more. It made me dream of the days we had spent roaming the woods together during our journey to Rock Hall, and it was déjà vu to spend the night up in the trees, where we had once slept together.

When our tour came to an end, I advised my companions to go ahead and return without me. I wanted to hang back for a while, since it was a particularly beautiful night. The sky was completely clear, revealing a galaxy of glittering stars. The other wolves had wanted to continue moving throughout the night but I... wanted to take a breather, and have some time with my own thoughts. On this night that so reminded me of the night I had first kissed my love.

My love. It was still hard to believe that was what Victoria had become for me. Ever since learning of my betrothal to Rona, I had come to believe that I would never experience such a miracle as love. I would either have to keep running forever and avoiding my marriage to Rona— remain celibate, or "single," as Victoria had referred to it— or be forced into a loveless marriage.

But now I had Victoria. My beautiful human girl.

After my comrades parted ways with me and disappeared into the trees to continue on their journey, I transformed into my humanoid form and swung up the nearest tree. I scaled higher and higher up the mighty trunk until my head emerged above the ocean of swaying leaves and I had full view of the spectacular sky.

I propped myself up on one of the thick branches and sat down, my back against the trunk, in a spot where my vision of the sky would not be impaired.

My nostalgia was stronger than ever up here. I closed my eyes, recalling the way Victoria's crystal-blue irises had reflected the starlight. I remembered her smile and the way she had looked afraid when I'd brought her into the treetops for the first time. Oh, how I wished that she was here with me now. What I wouldn't give to feel her weight on my lap, hold her in my arms… watch as she slowly fell asleep.

I let out a deep sigh and leaned my head back against the trunk. I opened my eyes again and gazed upward.

Love. It was such a strange thing, how it could be both bliss and agony at the same time.

My eyes glazed over as I continued to lose myself in

thoughts of my lover, wondering what she was doing right now, back in her island of eternal night. Whether she was thinking of me, too...

Then a streak of black caught my attention, directly above me. Normally such a thing would have barely caused me to pause. I would pass it off as a bird or something... but this streak of black had been large. Very large. It had raced across the sky so quickly it was a blur, and hurtled down toward a tree about a quarter of a mile away.

Could that have been a meteor? I had never witnessed meteors strike The Woodlands, but I had heard of such occurrences from other wolves.

Perhaps it was a meteor... A fallen star... A messenger from Victoria, reminding me that she loves me...

I fell back into my dreamy thoughts until I spotted it again. The same black streak, much closer to me this time. It streaked right across my vision and hurtled to my right. I stood up now, balancing on the branch and narrowing my eyes as I tried to make out what, exactly, it was.

And then I noticed something very strange indeed. The figure of a wolf. A black wolf? A huge black wolf. It looked at least twice my size.

What in the world...

Although my heart was pounding from the surprise, I couldn't help but move closer. As I moved from my tree to the next, the giant wolf drew closer to me, too, until we were both only twelve feet apart, staring at each other.

She was female—and the largest wolf I'd ever seen in my life. Far larger than I'd ever thought even existed. She had bright gray eyes... eyes that were bizarrely like mine.

As I breathed in to catch her scent, I experienced the strangest feeling. *Familiarity.* Like I knew that smell. Like I had scented it before. It was a feeling so deep inside of me that despite all logic telling me that it was impossible, my brain simply couldn't argue with it. I *felt* it. Somehow, somewhere, I had scented this wolf before.

She and I remained rooted to our spots, staring at each other for several moments. When she made no move to approach closer to me, I called out in a hoarse voice, "Who are you?"

I thought that I had either misheard her, or gone insane, when she replied, "I'm your mother, Bastien."

I had no words for about a minute. I just continued gaping at her. "What?" I stammered.

At this, she ventured closer until she had reached the branch directly opposite me—only five feet away. Her scent was almost overwhelming at this proximity. Especially since the evening breeze was blowing in our direction.

"You are my child. My long-lost son," she replied, in an unsteady voice. "Bastien Mortclaw is your real name. And I am Sendira Mortclaw."

"I... Y-You are mistaken," I choked. "I am Bastien Blackhall, and my mother is dead."

She moved closer still until she was sharing my branch. "Your mother was not who you thought she was," she replied softly. "She was a substitute for me."

"No," I said, shaking my head. "You are mistaken."

At this she cocked her head to one side. She looked almost wounded. "Do you not recognize me, son?"

I faltered. I couldn't deny it.

"But... But..."

Before I could continue with my stuttering, she suddenly morphed, and the next thing I knew, standing before me was a fully-clothed woman. Alarm rippled through me as I realized that she possessed the same power that I did—a power that I had not witnessed anybody else in The Woodlands ever possessing. The ability to turn at will, switch between man and wolf, be it night or day.

But what kind of magic was this— that she could appear fully clothed?

She was normal-sized in her humanoid form—not enlarged like she had been in her wolf form. And her appearance... I could see myself in her. Her curly black hair. Her gray eyes. She... she looked just like my mother ought to look. She looked more like my mother than my... other mother ever had.

"This is some kind of witchery," I breathed, backing away. "This *can't* be."

"My dearest," she said, her voice pained as she approached me. Her hands touched mine. "I can explain everything to you. Absolutely everything. If you will just hear me out..."

Here this woman was, holding my hands. She was not an apparition. She was real. How could I not hear her out?

"Come with me, and you will understand all the secrets of your past."

She shifted back into her giant wolf form and then lowered her head, gesturing that I climb onto her back. I hesitated for a moment, but again, how could I refuse?

I pulled myself on top of her back and then, without warning, she launched into the sky and flew at a speed that rivaled a dragon's—nay, a witch's.

I must have fallen asleep on that branch.

This can't be real.

This can't be.

She soared over the woods and headed toward the shore. She carried me several miles across the ocean until a cluster of rocks came into view. Here, she touched down. I had no idea why she wanted to talk to me here, but my mind was far too crowded with other questions to give it much thought.

I climbed off her back, my legs unsteady. She assumed her human form again and gestured that the two of us sit down on a rock.

We did. I couldn't stop staring at her face.

Then she began a story. A story that began at my birth. A story that involved kidnapping and "black witches". She said that when I was very young, still an infant, the black witches had taken all of the Mortclaw pack hostage due to their being the strongest, finest tribe in all The Woodlands. The Mortclaws had been taken away from The Woodlands and kept in solitude on an island, where the black witches had carried out all sorts of strange rituals on them. But they had managed to get me back to safety, via a kindly servant of the black witches who took pity on me and smuggled me out. I had been placed with a surrogate family back in my homeland and, even when the Mortclaws were freed from the black witches after the latter's demise, my parents had still not sought me out, for they had not wished to disturb me.

"Th-Then why are you here now?" I couldn't help but ask.

She drew in a breath. "I came across your substitute aunt, Brucella. We had been passing by The Trunchlands when I spotted her and her family. She informed me of your substitute parents' and siblings' deaths. I-I decided that now was the time to finally make myself known to you."

"Brucella?" I asked.

"Yes," she explained. "Your father and I were, uh, hunting by the ogres' island, and we happened to pass the Northstones on the shore."

My mind felt like it had been blown into a thousand pieces.

My whole life has been a lie. My parents, my siblings...
My gut twisted.

A part of me still wanted to deny it all. But as crazy as

everything sounded, I just couldn't help but believe her words now. My instincts had confirmed that this woman was my mother practically from the very moment I laid eyes on her, and now it was simply a question of my brain accepting it.

"And... my father? And do I have siblings?"

"You have no siblings, my beloved," she said, squeezing my hand gently. "But you have a father. A father who loves and misses you very much."

"Where is he?"

"We, um, decided that I ought to visit you alone at first, to see how you took to... everything I've told you. You understand?"

"Yes," I murmured, in a daze. "W-Why are you still so big? Why do you still have these strange powers?"

She shrugged wearily. "You are right that it is strange. We should have lost them when the black witches met with their demise... It remains a mystery to us why we still have the powers they bestowed upon us."

I fell into a stunned silence, everything she had just told me still sinking into my brain. I felt like I was bursting at the seams as I struggled to hold it all in at once. I could not find words again for a while... But as the minutes passed, there was something nagging me at the back of my mind. A nagging that wouldn't go away, despite my mother's explanation.

Brucella. She was the cause of my mother's seeking me out. Although I supposed it made sense that Brucella had made her way to the ogres' kingdom in search of me, it didn't sit right with me that she was the reason for my mother's sudden appearance. Even though I supposed that my foster parents' demise would've come up naturally enough in conversation between my so-called aunt and my mother, I had become so averse to Brucella that simply hearing her name put me in a suspicious mood. She did nothing without some expectation of return. Some hidden agenda… Would she really have sent my mother to me out of the goodness of her heart?

Still, it was my mother sitting in front of me. *My mother.* I should not let Brucella get in the way of that.

But then, as my mother slipped in a question, I couldn't help but prickle again: "I hear that you have a newfound mate?"

"Did Brucella tell you that?" I shot back, a little more tensely than I had intended.

She looked taken aback. "Why, yes. She told me a

number of things."

"Who did she say my mate was?" I asked, assuming that she would have been boastful and presumptuous enough to still be telling people that it was Rona.

"A-A human girl named Victoria," my mother replied.

My mouth dried out.

That *really* did not sit right with me.

I couldn't imagine Brucella saying such a thing. Admitting defeat already? Would she have? Might I have just tired her out by now? Or maybe Brucella had already found somebody for Rona, a replacement husband…

Whatever the case, I instinctively felt cagey when it came to talking about Victoria. I simply nodded and said, "Yes."

My mother paused, wetting her lower lip. "W-Would you care to describe her to me?"

I hesitated. "She's… she's very beautiful."

"Is she here with you in The Woodlands?"

I shook my head. "She's not here."

At this, my mother stopped asking questions about Victoria. She looked strangely tense.

We lapsed into silence again, falling back into just staring at each other again. There was a part of her that appeared to be just as disbelieving to see me as I was to see her.

"Well, Bastien," she said, rising slowly to her feet. "Perhaps we ought not make this first meeting too long. I-I understand you have a lot to think about and absorb now. I should probably return."

"Return where?" I asked.

"To Father," she replied. "We live... across the ocean."

I rose to my feet beside her. "Then I would like you to return me to The Woodlands," I replied.

"Of course." She moved forward tentatively and cupped my face in her hands. She leaned up to kiss me on both cheeks.

My mother. This really was my mother.

She reassumed her wolf form. I climbed onto her back, and she transported me back to The Woodlands with her bizarre, supernatural speed. She set me down in a clearing in the woods near Blackhall territory.

"I will come back to you soon, Bastien. I promise... I know where you live." She cast me a lingering glance.

I nodded at her, though somehow, I wasn't sure how to reply.

I watched as she launched into the sky again and

streaked away. And I remained standing and staring at the spot where she had disappeared.

My mother. She was my mother. And I have a father too. A family that is not dead but alive. A family that loves me.

So why am I not drunk with joy? Why am I not soaring? Why is my stomach knotted...

My foster mother had always said that I had uncanny instincts. That I sensed things a normal wolf would never sense. Sometimes it felt like it was a handicap. I became overly sensitive to things and overthought things far too much.

Maybe that was the case here.

Maybe it was just the shock of discovering her existence and in the morning I would feel very different.

She'd said that she would return to see me again. Maybe she would come with my father next time.

Maybe, after getting to know them, any uncertainty I felt would vanish.

Maybe I would even open up to them regarding Victoria. Maybe I would even want to introduce them to her, and explain that we were in love.

Hm.

Maybe...

READY FOR THE NEXT PART OF THE NOVAK CLAN'S STORY?

Dearest Shaddict,

The next book in the series is *A Shade of Vampire 29: An Hour of Need!* *An Hour of Need* releases **June 24th, 2016.**

Don't miss it!

Visit <u>www.bellaforrest.net</u> for details.

Here's a preview of the awesome cover:

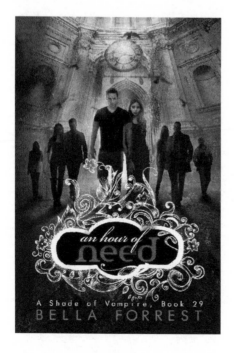

Thank you for reading, and I will see you again very soon!

Love,

Bella xxx

P.S. Join my VIP email list and I'll send you a personal reminder as soon as I have a new book out. Visit here to sign up: www.forrestbooks.com

(You'll also be the first to receive news about movies/TV show as well as other exciting projects that may be coming up!)

P.P.S. Follow The Shade on Instagram and check out some of the beautiful graphics: @ashadeofvampire

You can also come say hi on Facebook: www.facebook.com/AShadeOfVampire

And Twitter: @ashadeofvampire

Made in the USA
Lexington, KY
30 May 2016